Frédéric Ozanam, Pauline Stump

**A Pilgrimage to the Land of the Cid**

Frédéric Ozanam, Pauline Stump

**A Pilgrimage to the Land of the Cid**

ISBN/EAN: 9783337287375

Printed in Europe, USA, Canada, Australia, Japan

Cover: Foto ©Andreas Hilbeck / pixelio.de

More available books at **www.hansebooks.com**

# A PILGRIMAGE

## TO THE

# LAND OF THE CID.

*TRANSLATED FROM THE FRENCH*

OF

## FREDERIC OZANAM,

BY

*A Graduate of St. Joseph s, Emmittsburg.*

## NEW YORK:

CHRISTIAN PRESS ASSOCIATION PUBLISHING CO.,

1895.

# CONTENTS.

# THE LAND OF THE CID.

## BURGOS.

IT was a favorite devotion of our fathers to make a pilgrimage to St. James of Compostello. In the central parts of France, at Poitiers, for instance, the pilgrims to the shrine of St. James were sufficiently numerous in the last century to form a confraternity, which had a chapel a short distance from the city, on the road to Spain. Before returning to their homes, these pious travellers always visited the

beach where, about four leagues from
Compostello, says the legend, the body
of the holy apostle was washed ashore.
It was here they collected those large
shells that decorated their hats and
mantles, and which, when brought
home to the children, served as pas-
times to friends and neighbors during
the long winter evenings. I also
dreamed of a pilgrimage to St. James.
I rejoiced at the thought of seeing old
Christian Spain—that free, poor, neglected portion of Spain which bears
fewest traces of the stranger's foot-
steps. There were in store for me—
Burgos, the city of Our Lady, the
city of kings and heroes; Oviedo and
its valleys, unsullied by the Mussulman conquest; St. Iago, whose basi-

lica, though despoiled by revolutions, still retains the majesty of its gigantic architecture. But a Will which consults us not arrested my progress at the very first station, and my pilgrimage ended, not at the tomb of St. James, but in the country of the Cid. Hence I have returned with hands empty of shells, but filled with those light leaves whereon the traveller hastily traces his first impressions, vainly promising himself to retouch them later. These are all I can offer my friends and neighbors, to help while away their evenings, when, in a spirit of congeniality and Christian harmony, they gather around a common fireside, despite the blasts and storms without.

# I.

## THE PYRENEES AND THE SEA.

Gavarnie, Aug. 21—Biarritz, Sept. 1, 1852.

IN Italy, and upon the borders of Rhine, my thoughts were distracted by the works of man. Here, where man has done little, I see but the works of God. Truly, God is not only the great legislator, the great geometrician, he is also the great artist. Let us not despise poetry as the dream of weak imagination, or the pastime of an enervated age, for God himself is the author of all poetry. He has bounti-

fully scattered it throughout creation,
and if he decreed that the world-
work of his hands should be good, he
also decreed that it should be beautiful. What poet has ever conceived,
what architect has ever designed, a
sanctuary comparable to that which
the Eternal has built for himself in
the profoundest depths of the Pyrenees,
an isolated spot, where he is adored
by herdsmen only? It is called the
Circle of Gavarnie. But instead of a
circle, represent to yourself the apsis
of a temple, hewn out of rocks two
thousand four hundred feet high. On
reaching the base of these prodigious
walls, we saw their summits, tinged
with the roseate clouds of a setting
sun. which floated around them like

drapery, and, when the wind had dissipated these vapors, the heights of the edifice appeared crowned with eternal snows, under the blue pavilion of the firmament. Around us the voice of cascades moaned like an endless prayer. Here would I bring the atheist, to see him fall upon his knees, vanquished and enchanted by the grandeur of this unparalleled spectacle. Nothing approaches it in sublimity, unless, perhaps, the chaos through which one passes to reach it. Here enormous rocks, thirty, forty feet high, are piled up in indescribable magnificence from the summit of the mountain to the depths of the precipice, where roars the Gave. We might easily imagine this the scene of that combat described by Milton when good and evil spirits, contending, tore up the hills to hurl upon one another. But sights like these are rarer in the Pyrenees than the Alps. The Pyrenees have not the sublime horrors of a Mont Blanc; they have more elegance than majesty. Their chief beauties are the valley of Ossau, the valley of Argelès, and the Bridge of Spain. There are few glaciers, but laughing hillocks which kiss the limpid waters, sloping heights crowned with verdure, peaks towering towards heaven with marvellous grace, their crests of rose-tinted granite lost in the effulgence of a mid-day sun. Nowhere do we see more beautiful waters. They are not, it is true, the famed lakes of Switzerland; but Switzerland can boast of no such cascades; and there gushes not forth from the sides of her rocks such pure and abundant torrents. There is something suggestive of moral purity in these heights, seldom sullied by the foot of man; these waters quenching the thirst of the wild goat and eagle only; these flowers, blossoming but to perfume the solitude. David had just seen the heights of Lebanon when he exclaimed: "Wonderful is the Lord on high!" *Mirabilis in altis Dominus.*

Though these dwellers on the Pyrenees have not struggled boldly against their mountain-fastnesses, we must not imagine that their homes are mere mole-hills. Frequently a proud don-

jon confronts us, as if guarding the
entrance to these delightful valleys,
where our fathers trod less securely
than ourselves. All the caprices of
the Renaissance have decorated the
Castle of Pau; and the Ogive art has
never perhaps achieved more harmonious or beautifully lighted naves than
those of the Cathedral at Bayonne.
In this corner of the world there are
two historic antique peoples, the Béarnais and the Basques. On their festival days, especially, should we visit
these Béarnais, who glory in having
remained " pure. faithful, and courteous."
Whilst the surrounding provinces
gradually submitted to the ignominy of
the' blouse and pantaloons, these peasants of the valley of Ossau scrupu-

lously adhered to the costume of their
ancestors—the women still wearing the
capulet, which so gracefully veils their
modest heads; the men the berret, the
scarlet vest, the bright girdle, the short
breeches and gaiters—all investing their
wearers with an air of sprightly ease.
Never have I seen men more nimble
at the dance, as the musician, en-
throned upon the heights of a barrel,
executes a melancholy, monotonous air
upon a species of guitar, the four
strings of which he strikes with a
tampon, reminding us of the *cithara*
and the *plectrum* of the ancients.
Neither have I seen men more recol-
lected in the procession; and I sha'l
never forget the two long lines of
mountaineers who, upon the Eve of

the Assumption, slowly defiled upon Laruns Square, measuring their steps to the chant of hymns. I admired especially the dignified, majestic appearance of the old men, tall and straight as the pines of their native forests, and wearing those graceful mantles which are now seldom or never seen, except in pictures of the Middle Ages. Behind them came the Mayor and his assistants, habited like peasants, and with the official scarf fastened over their purple doublet. They are faithful rulers, we are assured, as skilful in meting out justice as in hunting the wild beasts of the mountain; and their fine open countenances, shaded by long hair, were true types of this noble, ingenuous race.

The Basque people have more gravity and less grace. It is certainly a pleasing spectacle to witness a match game of tennis between the youths of two cantons or villages, each side contending most spiritedly for the victory. The elders are constituted judges; and why should I conceal the fact that snugly stowed away in some cool retreat is the bottle, that unfailing counsellor in difficult cases? But still more zealously does each village strive to excel in the care of its cemetery; this place of mourning is planted thick with rose-bushes; a neglected grave is seldom seen; and no one enters the church without having first knelt upon the tomb of his ancestors to pray. Veneration for the dead is the mark of a healthful, moral race, clinging tenderly to its heritage of family pride and tradition. Every year, about a hundred of the Basques, tempted by the beautiful vessels anchored at Bayonne or the Passage emigrate to America to make their fortunes; but when enriched, they hasten homeward, sending out a younger brother to the same colonies, themselves quietly settling down in their native place, and decorating with their gifts the church, under whose shadow they will one day sleep beside their ancestors. Is it astonishing that these people religiously retain the language of their country, that their priests and learned men watch over it as a sacred fire, and that the

Basques of our day still speak the idiom of the old Iberians, those forefathers of the Germans and Celts, and one of the first peoples who left Babel to seek a westward course?

The mountains are all divine. They bear the imprint of the Hand that formed them. But what shall I say of the sea, or, rather, what shall I not say of it? Its grandeur strikes us at once; but we must contemplate it a long time ere recognizing that other ingredient of beauty which it possesses—grace. Homer understood this, and, though peopling ocean with terrible gods and monsters, he also made it the abode of nymphs and enchanting sirens. I have seen daylight die upon the Gulf of Gascogne, the sun sink-

ing behind the Cantabrian mountains,
whose bold outlines were clearly de-
fined against a sky of purest azure.
A golden, luminous mist, floating over
the waters, laved the mountains' feet,
whilst the never-resting surge, tinted
azure, green, lilac, rose, or purple
died away upon the sand, or dallied
with the rocks, which scattered the
white foam, just where the decomposed
light assumed the varied hues of the
rainbow. Sheafs of spray arose into
the air with all the elegance of those
artificial jets which decorate the gardens of kings, and here, in the do-
mains of God, these sports are eternal.
Each day they recommence; each day
they vary according to the strength
of the winds and height of the tide.

But these same waves, so caressing now. have hours of wrath, when, like the horses of the Apocalypse, they seem unchained, and their white squadrons are banded together in re-iterated attacks upon the dismantled cliffs defending the shore. Then, too, are heard terrible noises, as of the voice of the abyss demanding the prey snatched from it in the days of the deluge. Whilst the shore is thus ani- mated by ever changing scenes, the eye feasts upon that image of the In- finite. the open sea, immutable and boundless now as when the land was not, and the spirit of God moved upon the waters. David had admired this spectacle too, and perhaps from the heights of Carmel his glance embraced

the restless expanse of the Mediterranean, when he exclaimed with fervor,
" Wonderful are the surges of the
sea!" *Mirabiles elationes maris.*

All this may seem very solemn for
the beginning of a journey; but we
must not forget that a pilgrimage ever
commences with a psalm.

# II.

## ROAD TO ST. JAMES'.

ONE mild morning, the 16th of November, we crossed the Bidassoa and flew past the Isle of Pheasants. It is here the Peace of the Pyrenees was signed, and though now half submerged by the gradually-encroaching waters, neither France nor Spain has ever lifted a hand to its rescue. Our route lay along the Guipuzçoa. On one side arose the abrupt peaks, the woody declivities, and the cultivated hills

22

connecting the Pyrenees with the Asturias, whilst, on the other, at frequent intervals, we caught glimpses of the sea. Its magnificent scenery, its salubrious air, its verdure, still fresh and lively at a season so far advanced, make the country a terrestrial paradise, but a paradise stained with blood by the passions of men, as we readily perceive from the yet distant view of Fontarabia's castle and dismantled bastions. Let us not dream of slighting this small but valiant city. We enter it—as is fitting one should enter Spain —by ruins, through crumbling ramparts and a tottering gate. Stretching out before us is a street, the most Spanish this side of Toledo, all bordered with ancient houses, with their balconies, their galleries, their lattices whence the ladies within see and are seen, their doors bearing armorial devices. At the end of this street arise two noble edifices, the castle of Charles V., whose dark cyclopean mass has been grazed by many a bullet, and the church, which alone remains intact in the midst of this dilapidated city, as if reminding us that the God of ruins is also the God of resurrections. But Fontarabia does not sleep amidst her desolation. The sardine fishers here form a numerous class—proud of the purity of their blood and the chastity of their daughters; and the palaces are not mere deserted ruins, but ruins resounding with the joyous sounds of life and happiness.

A few miles from Fontarabia the cliffs along the coast open, and with the receding hills help form the port of the Passage—that Gibraltar of the north, which will be to regenerated Spain a secure harbor for her reconstructed navy. We have now reached the rich village of Renteria, whose fruitful apple orchards are worthy of a Normandy farm. From thence a long causeway brings us to the gates of St. Sebastian. What more picturesque and beautiful spot than this city at the foot of the mountain, and enclosed upon three sides by the sea? Why should those old Biscayan habitations, burned and razed by the English, ever have given place to these monotonous streets, laid cut with the precision of a cord, and every house presenting the same jaundiced front? Wholly detached from this perspective are the two churches of the Blessed Virgin and St. Vincent, their lofty arches reposing upon elegant pillars of the Renaissance. St. Vincent already possesses one of those magnificent altar-pieces which constitute the boast of Spanish churches, and which, reaching to the very roof, are a religious epic of pictures, a paradise of sculptures. Nor can I forget the market-place, animated by groups of vigorous men, and women with long plaits reaching to their heels. Here the fruits of the country and wines in leathern bottles are brought in upon ox-teams whose solid spokeless wheels are no bad representation of the chariots of Alaric and Attila. As the alguazil makes his rounds among the arcades, all dressed in black, the tri-cornered hat upon his head, a mantle upon his shoulders, knee-breeches decorating his extremities, he might easily be mistaken for an officer of the Holy Inquisition.

On leaving St. Sebastian, we turn our faces from the sea, and soon enter a valley like those of the Lower Pyrenees, still verdant, and watered by a rapid stream. Here we find the same Basque people with its industry and activity. Not a foot of ground upon these heights is lost, and the villages are not only numerous but

well-built. Here we see a rope-walk
or a forge; there, the house of a returned emigrant who, having made his
fortune in America, is henceforth styled
the Indian. The large town of Tolosa marks the first round of this
giant's ladder we are about to ascend.
Beyond, the country grows less smiling, the route more rugged, yet our
mules speed along at a fine pace.

Who has not heard of the Spanish
teams, of the long line of mules har-
nessed two by two, and which the
mayoral, from his elevated seat, man-
ages both dextrously and boldly?—not,
however, without animating them by
a continued conversation, by flattering
names and pathetic cries: " Brava,
Capitana! Adelante, Catalana! Ani-

mo, Pastora!" So vigorous were the
gestures and voice that Pastora fel
upon his side, and was raised only by
repeated blows of the whip. O country of Garcilaso and Montemayor—
classic land of eclogue! how can you
bear such profanation of the names of
your shepherdesses? At last, our
awkward nags were reinforced by
oxen, and we made the rude passage
of Salinas. Night veils the flourish-
ing city of Vitoria, and day surprises
us at Miranda on the Ebro, upon the
frontiers of old Castile. We might
easily imagine ourselves upon the
frontiers of Siberia.

We must figure Spain to ourselves
as an immense mountain, whose base
is plunged in hot or tepid waters, and

whose summit is a vast plain, furrow-
ed in turn by other mountains. This
plateau forms the two Castiles, Estra-
madura, and La Mancha, elevated two
thousand feet above the ocean, and
devoured, in turn, by sultry suns and
freezing blasts. The Spaniards say,
"Six months hell and six months
winter." The latter season had com-
menced, and instead of the warm
breezes which yesterday caressed the
Bay of Biscay, we now felt the breath
of snow and frosts.

The landscape was chill and gloomy.
On the east, as far as the eye could
reach, a naked country devoid of trees
and bare of crops; to the west, two
mountain chains, whose dark and rugged profiles were traced against a

cloudy sky; at our feet, the Ebro, rolling its waters with the rapidity of a torrent, and at both ends of the bridge which crosses this river the streets of Miranda, narrow, miserable, and choked with filth and rags. The church of St. Nicholas with its Roman arch, its low and humble nave, its dimly-lighted windows, recalls most forcibly that period of Spanish history when the Christians, poor and few in number, less occupied with building than battling, still disputed this spot of earth with the infidels.

Groups of animated figures relieved the monotony of the scene. Herdsmen, habited in sheepskins, and driving before them those migratory flocks which annually descend from the Sierra

Nevada to the Pyrenees; muleteers, with their glittering girdles and embroidered vests, a gaudily-colored woollen wrapping thrown over their shoulders; beggars, draped in their tatters, with less grace but more pride than the Italians. These people bear not the slightest resemblance to those of the Basque provinces. We are now in the midst of a brave and original, but poverty-stricken, indolent race—Castilians noble as the king, and too proud to lift a hand if they have but bread—"the good old Castilians," *Castellanos rancios y viejos.*

The first glimpse of the country is not at all enchanting. Here those two mountain-chains, bounding the eastern and western horizon, approach and en-

close our route between two walls of
solid rocks, whose summits appear as
if rent asunder by a thunderbolt. This
is the gorge of Pancorbo, tinted with
the blood of the infidels in the ninth
century. The ruins of a castle over-
look the desolated town. One might
easily imagine war to have passed but
lately over these ruined villages, these
houses without windows, often without
doors, though built of immense stones,
as if to sustain a siege. Yet this
melancholy, dangerous road was the
one most frequented by French or
Italian pilgrims to St. James of Compostello. How many miserable human
beings have journeyed hither in tears,
seeking the remission of their sins,
the healing of a malady, the deliver-

ance of a captive! and through what
perils, when Saracen bands scoured the
country, and encroaching waters destroyed the bridges and crossings. We
read in the legend of St. Bonne, a
virgin of Pisa, that on one occasion,
making a pilgrimage to St. James
with a large number of the faithful,
reunited by a common danger, she
stopped on reaching the banks of a
torrent, the bridge over which was too
unsafe to cross. "Lift up your arms
towards heaven, and pass over," said
Christ, appearing to the saint. As
she set foot upon the tottering beams,
all her companions exclaimed in ter-
ror: "Oh! trust it not; you will surely
be drowned!" But at that moment a
multitude of saints descended from

heaven; popes, bishops, with mitre
and all the insignia of their sacerdotal
rank, ranged themselves each side of
the bridge, whilst the pilgrim crossed
in safety. When she had gained the
other side, Christ spoke to her again.
"Call thy companions," said he, "for
none of them shall perish if thou stand-
est with uplifted hands as they cross."
Some of them hesitated; but one whose
pure eyes were allowed to penetrate
the mysteries of heaven, declaring she
saw the bright hosts of popes and
bishops, boldly advanced, and was followed by the whole band.

We pilgrims of the present day
need a celestial guard no less than
our brethren of the eleventh century.
The carabineers of the Spanish queen,

who have been our escort since yesterday, are a much greater source of
alarm than protection, for they carry
with them seventeen millions of
reals, and over a road where almost
any evening one would not be sur-
prised to see half a dozen carbines
spring up from behind a bush. Yet
this solitude is peopled, historic names
succeed one another all along the
route. Leaving behind us the mountains of Auca, whose bishops held a
seat in the first councils of Spain,
we reach the walled enclosure of
Briviesca, where King John the First
convoked the Cortes in 1388, and at
last the rich hamlet of Gamonal,
which announces the approach to
Burgos, whose cathedral spires, now

visible, publicly proclaim the descent of Christian inspiration upon this indigent, arid land.

# III.

## THE CITY OF HEROES.

Burgos, Nov. 18, 1852.

THE first glimpse of Burgos is not at all imposing. We enter through a faubourg along the left bank of the Arlanzon, like all other faubourgs thick with inns and warehouses, and presenting nothing peculiarly Spanish except the church belfries and a few houses with balconies across from the upper stories. A stone bridge, securely built upon the river's capricious bed, con-

ducts us to the right bank. Here
the city of Burgos spreads out before us with all the appurtenances of
the metropolis of a second-class province; a large quay, bordered with
sickly-looking stunted trees; farther
on, the Grand Square, surrounded by
porticoes, continually thronged with
groups of young and old Castilians,
as proudly wrapped in their indolence as their mantles. Behind the
square extends Dove Street, poetic
and deceitful name of the mercan-
tile quarter, where all national imprint is effaced beneath the progress
of European civilization. Here the
houses have doors and windows almost intact, and even chimneys. But,
if you possess a romantic spirit and

are enamored of ruins, be consoled; this apparent prosperity conceals only abandoned streets and deserted places, where a little rubbish guards a great name. Let us take for our guide one of these children in tatters; I cannot guarantee that he will refuse your maravedis, but rest assured he will be proud to show you the city of heroes.

To the north of the modern city, and as we redescend towards the west, arise the antique walls, half destroyed, but still extensive and formidable in appearance, crowned with battlements and pierced with gates, whose horse-shoe arches recall the days of the Moors. Tradition, like the ivy, clings around these ruins. It is said that, in 884, a Christian chief, Diego Porcellos, having defeated the Saracens in the gorges of Pancorbo, built this enclosure for the protection of the women, children, and booty, and gave it the Germanic appellation Burgos (*burg*, castle). This son of the Goths wished to ally his race with the blood of the North, and his daughter, Sulla Bella, married a German nobleman who had come hither on a pilgrimage to St. James of Compostello, but who remained for the pious purpose of combating the infidel. From this union descended, though in different degrees, Nuño de Rasura, the Count Fernan Gonzalez, the seven children of Lara, and the Cid. In this way the legend unites

in one line all the heroes of Castile, and by thus making their genealogy date back to the most obscure
periods, it seeks to enfranchise them
from the feudalships of the kings.
The ancient rivalry between the
dukedom of Castile and the kingdom of Leon seems to have been
coeval with their existence as politi-
cal provinces, and we learn from the
history of this remote age that the
princes of Leon always wielded a
very unstable authority at Burgos.
But the legend takes care to make
them sever the bond by a crime. Or-
doño II., inviting the Castilian chiefs
to a banquet, puts them to death.
To avenge their injuries the in-
sulted people rise up against their

kings, and summon them to judgment. Nuño de Rasura and Lain Calvo ruled in Burgos, as Joshua and Gideon formerly in Israel. Nothing is now known of their government, but how can we doubt their existence, when we are shown, in one of the rooms of the ayuntamiento, the wooden chair, low and without ornament, from which they pronounced sentence according to the laws of the nation?*

A monument of larger size, but less characteristic, marks the spot where

---

* For this and the following account I have made frequent reference to a recent and instructive notice, *Apuntes sobre Burgos* published in this city, and embellished with correct and tasteful illustrations.

once stood the house of Fernan Gonzalez. Who would beieve that Philip II., that distrustful monarch, had erected this triumphal arch in honor of the great Count of Castile, who was often seen armed against the infidels, but always sword in hand against the kings? The ballads proclaim him the indomitable chief, who one by one conquered all the castles around Burgos, repulsing the Mussulmans to the west, the Navarrais to the north, and in the tenth century reuniting all Castile in one free and hereditary dukedom. Heaven seconds him against the infidels, and the love of his wife against his Christian enemies. At Piedrahita he battles three consecutive days without gaining any

advantage over the infidels, when at
last the Apostle St. James appears,
battling in his behalf, mounted upon
a white courser, and armed with a
glittering sword, which, striking right
and left, soon decides the victory.
Twice betrayed by the kings of Navarre and Leon, and cast into their
castle dungeons, Fernan Gonzalez twice
escapes through the artifices of his
wife, Doña Sancha, and the devotion
of his people. At the news of his
captivity all the men of Burgos rise
up in his defence, "and all took an
bath with one voice not to enter Castile without their lord the count—if he
returns not, neither will they; and pre-
ceded by his image, carved in stone,
and mounted upon a chariot, like

faithful vassals they slowly journey towards the Arlanzon, measuring their course by the sun." The Castilians wishing to free themselves from the feudal tribute they owed Leon, their great count resolved to effect it. Summoned to attend the Cortes of Leon, he boldly repairs thither, banishing all thoughts of that prison where he had languished so long. He was mounted upon a horse of fabulous price, and upon his wrist a magnificent falcon. The king, coveting these superb animals, offers him a fixed sum, to be paid a certain day, and doubled for each day the payment is delayed. The bargain having been concluded, a dispute arises between them, and when, after several years of war, the victorious Fernan demands a strict compliance with the articles of the agreement, the appointed umpires, seeing that all the treasures of the kingdom would not suffice to cancel the debt, give him in exchange the absolute independence of his dukedom. "The count held his debtor to the agreement, for it irked him sorely to kiss another man's hand, and he returned thanks to God for having delivered glorious Castile from the allegiance of Leon." Thus chants the Spanish ballad. How willingly nations mingle ruse and heroism with their origin! Carthage preserves the remembrance of the beef-hide that marked her site, and all Greece places the cunning Ulysses beside Achilles.

If, now, your juvenile guide, more, anxious to follow up the legend than save your steps, conduct you to the solitary height where the arch of Fernan decorates the Cathedral Square, you will see just at the entrance of this noble edifice a line of trunkless heads. This sinister ornament represents the seven heads of the seven children of Lara. Do not fear that because I have just bought *The True Account of the Seven Children of Lara* at a corner of the herb-market, from a ballad dealer surrounded by a numerous patronage of muleteers, I am going to inflict upon you this long story from beginning to end. I shall remark only that the scene opens like that of Niebelungen, by a dispute between two women at a wedding-feast. Doña Lambra, wishing to be revenged upon the spouse and seven sons of her rival, soon succeeds by her artifices in betraying Gonzalo Bustos de Lara, the loyal chevalier, into the hands of Almanzor, king of Cordova. Here he remains a captive, though treated with the respect due his rank. Meanwhile, his seven sons being treacherously enticed into an ambuscade, and succumbing to superior numbers, are slain, and their trunkless heads sent to Cordova. At Almanzor's table is seated Gonzalo de Lara, for this illustrious lord is truly worthy of eating with kings. After the usual courses are served, "Friend Gonzalo," says the king, "a

very dainty dish is wanting." "At
your table, my lord," replies the noble
hidalgo, uncovering his venerable white
locks, "there is no lack of anything."
A basin is now brought in, covered
with a napkin, which, when removed,
discloses a ghastly sight—seven heads,
dead branches of this despoiled trunk.
Gonzalo, contemplating it, says: "Ah,
precious fruits! who has transported you
from Burgos to the fields of the infidel?"

Every one knows the rest of the
story, and how Mudarra, a half brother,
revenged their death. The citizens of
Burgos still show the tower whence
the author of so many evils, Doña
Lambra, precipitated herself in despair, and to this day it is called the
Tower of the Suicide.

But these warlike legends are only preludes to the Castilian epic. All the genius of old Castile is concentrated in the history of the Cid. The action begins at Burgos, the paternal abode of heroes, and finishes near there, at the national sanctuary of St. Peter of Cardena. In a deserted street, once resounding with the noise of men and horses, a pillar of stone between two small obelisks marks the site of the house where this invincible warrior was born. The inscription reads thus:

En este sitio estuvo la casa y nació el año MXXVI Rodrigo Diaz de vivar llamado, el Cid Campeador.

If the *Chronicles* of the Cid appear to fix his hereditary fief in the burg of Vivar, the ballads also give him possessions in the city. It was here, no doubt, he swore to avenge the outrage upon his old father; and here, too, he brought Ximena, on leaving the castle of Burgos, where his nuptials were celebrated; and here also the noble lady sighed for her warrior's return.

En los solares de Burgos,
A su Rodrigo aguardando.

A few steps farther and we are at the Church of St. Agatha (Sant' Agueda), renovated in the fifteenth century, but whose narrow nave recalls the proportions of the first Spanish basilicas. St. Agatha, however, was a highly venerated sanctuary, one of the three *iglesias juraderas,* or churches where the accused cleared themselves by oath. Cross the threshold, and you assist at the second act of the Spanish poem—the struggle between the king and the Cid. The independence of Castile, achieved by Fernan Gonzalez, lasted only a century. The princes of Leon, securely established in Burgos, extended their regal prerogatives across the country, levying tribute and forcing the nobles to feudal service. On their side, the *ricos hombres* entrenched themselves behind a bulwark of defiance and jealousy. The struggle between king and nobles in Spain commences as it did in Greece, the dispute between Alphonso VI. and the Cid reminding one forcibly of that between Achilles and Agamemnon. But

the wrath of the Cid is a just, Christian anger—it breaks forth in a church
and not without grave cause. Alphonso
VI., accused by public rumor of having
put to death his own brother, Don
Sancho, is required to prove his inno-
cence. "And the day the king took
oath at St. Agatha's, the Cid, taking
in his hands the book of the Holy
Gospels, placed it upon the altar.
Then King Alphonso put his hand on
the book, and the Cid interrogated
him in these terms: 'King Alphonso,
you are here to swear concerning the
death of the king Don Sancho, your
brother, that you neither killed him
yourself nor know anything about the
murder. Say 'I swear it,' you and
these other hidalgos." The king and

his hidalgos responded: 'We swear it.'*
Then the Cid continued: 'If you are
in any wise implicated in this deed,
may you die the death of the king
Don Sancho, your brother! May a
villain kill you, and not a scion of
noble blood! May he spring from
a foreign land, and not Castile!'
The king and his nobles answered,
"Amen,'" but when required by the
Cid to repeat this oath thrice, the second time the king changed color, the
third time he was greatly irritated
against the Cid, and henceforth there
was strife between them Tradition,
which not unfrequently degenerates in
the course of ages, has spoiled this,

* We here recognize the *conjuratores* of the
ancient Germanic laws.

beautiful narration, by clothing it with an air of superstition, in making the accused swear, not upon the Gospels, but upon a bolt which is still shown at the church door.

Alphonso VI. did not smother his resentment, and one day meeting the Cid between Burgos and Vivar, "Ruy Diaz," said he, "depart from my lands." Putting spur to his horse, the Cid leaped upon his patrimonial estate, and answered: "My lord, I am not on your lands, but my own." The king replied, greatly exasperated: "Depart from my kingdom, and without delay." And here begins the Cid's exile. It is at Burgos we must read the account, near that Moorish gate through which he passed, and these ruined walls, towards which he turned his longing eyes. We must read it in *The Poem of the Cid*, more ancient than the *Romances*, more ancient than the *Chronicle*, and beginning with its hero's disgrace.

"My Cid Ruy Diaz entered Burgos. He led into the field sixty banners. Men and women throng to see him. The people of Burgos are at their windows, weeping most bitterly, so deep is their grief, and in every mouth is the same lamentation: 'Oh! what a good vassal, had he but a good master!' Yet no one dares invite him in. The Campeador goes towards his dwelling; it is securely closed; and though his attendants call out in a loud voice, there is no re-

sponse from within. Leaping from his
horse, the Cid himself tries the gate,
he knocks, but in vain. At last a little
girl about nine years of age appears.
'Campeador,' says she, 'blessed be the
hour when you girded on the sword!
But we cannot open to you. Yesterday
evening came the king's letter, closely
sealed, and attended with all solemnity.
On no account must we lodge or entertain you, unless we wished to lose
our houses, our possessions—the very
eyes out of our heads. Cid, our woes
would benefit you not; but may the
Omnipotent Creator lend you his aid!'
Saying this, she withdrew into the
house. The Cid now saw there was
nothing to be hoped from the king;
so, turning away, he hastened towards

St. Mary's, where, dismounting, he entered and knelt in fervent prayer. Then, leaping upon his horse, he passed through the city gate, and was soon on the banks of the Arlanzon. Here, not far from the city, he pitched his tent." *

When our exile knelt at St. Mary's, ere turning his face toward the river, the humble church was still far from that splendor which it attained under the auspices of St. Ferdinand, when its walls were extended, its arches raised, and its modest exterior transformed into Our Lady of Burgos. Yet the magnificent cathedral piously guards the memory of the humiliated

* *Poema del Cid* v. 15

hero who knelt before its altar. In
one of the capitulary rooms is suspended a great chest, like the reliquary of a saint. Beneath is the Cid's
portrait, encased in iron, as if in veri-
fication of the account which follows.
In vain did he depart from his fief
accompanied by sixty banners. He
and his followers must have food.
Then the Cid, taking aside his nephew,
Martin Antolinez, sent him to Burgos,
with a message for two Jews, Rachel
and Bidas, with whom he had been
accustomed to traffic in booty, requesting them to return with Antolinez to
the camp. Meanwhile, two large iron-
cased coffers, each with a triple lock,
and so heavy that four men could
scarcely raise one even when empty

are filled with sand, and the surface
covered with gold and precious stones.
The Jews, on their arrival, are shown
these coffers, and the Cid tells them
that, not wishing to be encumbered with
the charge of such enormous treasures
in camp, that he entrusts them to their
keeping, requesting them to lend him
upon them a certain sum, of which he
stands in need. And the Jews lend
him three hundred marks of gold and
the same amount of silver. "But
when the Cid took Valencia he re-
deemed his chests of sand, by returning the three hundred marks of gold,
and the three hundred marks of silver,
and asked pardon of Rachel and Bidas, for it had grieved him sorely to
have been guilty of such a decep-

tion."* This last trait touches me. I believe the Castilian delighted to have played such a trick upon two infidels, but surely his Castilian honor suffered in consequence, and necessitated an apology.

The Achilles of Spain did not lead a life of indolence and ease beneath his tent ; his lance, henceforth free and sovereign, was poised against the infidel.  He cannot rest until he has besieged Valencia, "the honor and joy of the Moors, the city of strong walls, whose white battlements are seen from afar glittering in the sun!" The siege is long and the famine cruel.* The father no longer

* *Cronica del Cid*, cap. xc. and ccxiv. I here return to the *Chronicles*, as the account is more condensed.

advises with his son, nor the son with his father, nor friend with friend : they have no hope and no source of consolation. Oh! there is nothing worse than to want bread, to see one's wife and children die of hunger."* The poem follows Rodriguez in his conquests. We go to meet him at the term of all earthly grandeur, the tomb, chosen by himself not far from his ancestral patrimony. About two leagues southeast of Burgos is the abbey of St. Peter of Cardena, the oldest community of St. Benedict's order in Spain, and founded

* Quotation from an Arabic lament upon the taking of Valencia, and first published in the preface of *Cancionero de Baena*.

by a princess of the royal race of Goths in 537, as a resting-place for the remains of her son. It is a glorious house, and failed not to take part in the national struggle against the Saracens. In 872, falling into their hands, the infidels pillaged it, and massacred under its cloisters the Abbot Stephen with two hundred of his monks. In 899 it was rebuilt by Alphonso III., but tradition says that for six hundred years after, on the anniversary of the massacre, the martyr's blood reappeared on the stones where it had been shed, and that this annual miracle never ceased until 1492, when the taking of Granada washed away for ever the Christians' injuries. This was a favorite spot of the Cid's. On going into exile, it was to the Abbé of Cardena he confided his wife Ximena and his two daughters, and at St. Peter's of Cardena did he desire sepulture. At his death his widow and her friends brought him hither from Valencia, embalmed, girded in armor, and seated upon his horse, and here too they deposited their precious charge, not recumbent in a tomb like common mortals, but seated upon a stool, enveloped in his mantle, and sword in hand. Four years after, Doña Ximena lay at his feet "And when the good horse Babieça died, the groom to whose charge he had been entrusted, not wishing to bury him within the mon-

astery enclosure, dug him a grave to
the right of the gate, planting over
it two English elms, one at the head
and one at the foot, and these trees
grew to a great size." Still later,
King Alphonso X. erected in the
church choir a tomb to the Cid
bearing the following inscription,
which savors more of the soldier
than the great scholar:

" Belliger, invictus, famosus morte, triumphis,
   Clauditur hoc tumulo magnus Didaci Rodericus."

But time has not spared this
monument. The Benedictines of Cardena removed it from the choir to
the sacristy, from the sacristy to the
choir, and thence to the chapel of
St. Sisebut. Meantime, the vandalism
of modern improvement disfigured the

church, and a great wonder it is
that the equestrian statue of the Cid
at the entrance, crushing a Saracen
under his horse's feet, was ever left
standing. The honored exile seems
destined never to find an asylum
against the caprices of men. The
French carried off his tomb to Burgos as a decoration for the public
promenade. The restoration replaced
it in the vaults of St. Peter, and at
last, when a law of violence opened
the convent gates, the governor of
Burgos, fearing lest some English
tourist should carry off the bones
of Rodriguez and Ximena, now left
unguarded, placing the precious remains in a walnut coffin, removed
them from the antique abbey to the

chapel of the city hospital. With the
deepest melancholy, though not without some doubts as to their authenticity, did I contemplate these remains, exhibited for the sum of twc
reals by an attendant, who removed
the funeral pall and opened the coffin.
I have a horror of this violation
of the secrets of death, and I shud-
der at sight of these dried bones, at
least when sanctity has not covered
them with her imperishable vestments. The Church herself respects
this feeling, and when exposing to
our veneration the relics of the
saints, she encases them in gold,
and hides them beneath a veil
of crystal or a cloud of incense.

Three hundred years ago the magis-

trates of Burgos honored their heroes
indeed. When the battle of Villalar
had ruined the cause of the *comuneros*,
in whose behalf Burgos had drawn
her sword, that city, wishing to appease the wrath of Charles V., erected
in his honor a triumphal arch. But to
show at the same time that she had
lost nothing of her pride, this monument of her submission was also a com-
memoration of her most ancient glories Do not accuse me again of
stopping at mere inscriptions or masses
of stones heaped up regardless of art,
If we except the cathedral, Burgos
contains no edifice more striking than
this, none more truly inspired with
the old Castilian spirit, none more
redolent of classic tradition. At the

extremity of the quay, on the right
bank, and just opposite the bridge
arises a feudal gate, between two
prominent towers of a severe and
ornate style.    In niches immediately
above the grand arch are statues
of the founder of the city, Diego Porcellos, and the Castilian judges, Nuño
de Rasura and Lain Calvo; and above
these again, the statue of Charles V.
upon an elevated pedestal; at his right
and left, the great Count Fernan Gonzalez and the Cid, his good sword in
hand, and upon his breast the long
flowing beard so often the theme of
poet's song.    Still above the great
emperor, and as if reminding us of a
power superior to that of kings, is the
figure of an angel, armed with an ex-

terminating sword. And at the summit
of the edifice between the four cre-
nated arches which crown it, is the
Virgin and her Child—a forcible re-
minder that grace is even more powerful than the sword.*

---

\* This perhaps is the proper place for delineating
that fabulous genealogy which reunites the Castilian heroes in one family, as St. Mary's arch reunites their images in one monument.

DOM DIEGO PORCELLOS.

His daughter
SULLA BELLA
was mother of two sons.

| NUNO RASURA, Judge of Castile, | | GUSTIO GONZALEZ, |
| --- | --- | --- |
| his son, | From his daughter, | ancestor of |
| NUNO FERNANDEZ, | married to | the seven children |
| was father of | LAIN CALVO, | of LARA. |
| FERNAN GONZALEZ. | descended | |
| | DIEGO LAINEZ, | |
| | father of the CID. | |

These were the heroic days of Castile—in all their vigor and rudeness, it is true, yet tempered by the gentleness of Christianity. I here notice three striking traits; and first, the religious spirit which animated the war against the infidels, for I fear we do not sufficiently appreciate those prodigies of devotion and perseverance at the price of which alone was the Christian nationality saved, "when," according to the expression of an ancient chronicler, "the struggle against the Moors was at its height—those fearful times when kings, counts, nobles, and chevaliers lodged their horses in the same chamber with themselves and wives, so that if awakened by the battle-cry, they could mount at once and fly to the fray. Afterwards followed the passion for independence, not only personal independence, but that of all Castile. It is this that embroils the judges, the counts, Fernan Gonzalez, and the Cid in a perpetual struggle with the King of Navarre and Leon. We must not consider these nobles, as is too frequently done, utterly rebellious subjects, malcontents, enemies of all law and order; on the contrary, they constituted themselves defenders of the ancient laws, of the *fueros,* which the people strove to preserve intact against Alphonso X., his legislators, and his code of *Siete partidas.* And lastly, I admire the domestic affections in all their simplicity and energy, a brother's hand revenging the seven children of Lara, a wife's devotion twice breaking the chains of Fernan· Gonzalez. The Cid, as a son, wiping out his father's shame; as a husband, faithfully preserving to Ximena the battle-stained hand he had pledged her; as a father, following up the injuries of his children. The poem gives us a beautiful account of the banished hero's farewell to his family on leaving St. Peter of Cardena. "He clasped his two daughters in his arms, weeping over them most bitterly. 'Ah! Ximena, my peerless wife,' said he, 'I love you as my own soul. But you yourself see that in this world we must part. I must go and you remain! May it please God and the Holy Mary that

my arms may one day be able to en-
fold my daughters again. May it
please God to bless 'my fortunes,' that
you, my honored wife, may once more
enjoy a husband's protection!' My
Cid and his wife went to the church;
Doña Ximena knelt upon the altar
steps, beseeching the Creator most
fervently to protect the Cid Campeador. 'Thou art the King of kings,
said she, 'and Father of the world. I
adore Thee, and I believe in thee
with all my heart; and I beg the
holy St. Peter to pray also for my
Cid Campeador. May God preserve
him from evil! Since we must part
to-day, let it not be for ever!' Mass
was over, and the moment of separa-
tion had come The Cid embraces

Doña Ximena, and Doña Ximena, weeping bitterly, kisses his hand, for she knows not what to do. Then, tenderly regarding his daughters, 'I commend you to God, my children,'—said he—'to God, your mother, and your spiritual father.'" Thus they parted, as the nail from the flesh. We find here none of that sickly senti-mentality which characterizes the pro-ductions of the Troubadours. Nature needs not the trappings of art and ex-cessive refinement. Her simplest cries are enough to move men's hearts. We recognize also the accents of that parting between Hector and Andro-mache, though with the added lustre of Christian 'majesty—at least, that grace and beauty of which the Greek muse possesses the secret; for in the poem of the Cid, as in the Homeric epics, we approach the original fount of all poesy. Homer's works give back the sound of those warlike chants which he has collected, transformed, and revivified; and even so is the Castilian epic of the thirteenth age an echo of those unwritten songs extolling the already invincible Rodriguez:

" Ipse Rodericus, mio Cid semper vocatus,
  De quo cantatur quod ab hostibus haud supera-
    tur."

We can penetrate no further into the origin of Spanish literature. It is from such pure and simple beauties that a grand literature springs, even as great empires arise from the strong foundations of morality and purity.

But whilst wandering among ruins and memories, I perceive that my friends begin to grow anxious. No doubt you have heard Spain slandered, and fear lest on our return from so many jaunts I should find little better lodgings and cheer than the Cid and his companions upon the banks of the Arlanzon. But let me defend this beautiful and much-abused country. If here we cannot admire such hotels as those of Paris or London—where modern hospitality fleeces its visitors—we at least sleep under honest roofs and upon decent couches, and though the chambers are thoroughly rural, the kitchens are grand indeed. Never have I seen suspended from any ceiling a larger collection of dripping-pans, saucepans, and kettles. My eye was particularly attracted by the long line of pots, reminding me (pardon this Homeric allusion once more) of the long row of Penelope's servants, whom Telemachus, in punishment of their perfidy, suspended from one rope. Projecting into the middle of the room are the mantel-piece and patriarchal chimney, where the wet and benumbed traveller finds a welcome, without fear of horrifying a host of cooks accustomed to the happy familiarity of Spanish manners. His eyes will be consoled by the tempting sight of fried eggs, partridges gilded by a clear fire, and brown, foaming chocolate. If you are content with this, if you dread not the excessive perfume which gives the seal of authenticity to a flagon of Malaga, and if your stom-ach has not the dangerous curiosity to try the dried peas soaking in the adjoining hut, or meats dressed with rancid oil, throw aside your fears—we shall live; and you will not regret that I descended from my poetic heights to these useful realities. We have not actually forsaken the realms of Spanish literature; for if the poem of the Cid had its birth on the battle-field, it was from the kitchen of an inn that Don Quixote sallied forth to combat giants and redress wrongs.

# IV.

## THE CITY OF KINGS.

Burgos, November 19, 1852.

CRITICS, always inveighing against a traveller's enthusiasm, will accuse me of having admired Spain by the light of its legends and the illusions of its sun. I hasten to protest against the accusation. Four times have I seen day break upon the horizon of old Castile, but never have I seen that luminary which ushers in the day. I am, alas! among the number of those who come hither seeking health, seek-

ing it under skies too vaunted. The
poets, however, had warned me of this.
Ought I to be astonished at the snows
of Rome and the Tiber's swelling
waters when Horace, centuries ago,
reproached Jupiter for his perpetual
frosts, and complained that in the
reign of Augustus he saw once more
the deluge of Deucalion? * And when
Dante, in the third circle of his *Inferno*, describes the rain, "eternal,
cursed, cold, and sad,"

"Eterna, maladetta, fredda e grave," †

he certainly drew his imagery
from the banks of the Arno at Pisa,

---

* Horace, *Od.*, lib. 1 :
  "Jam satis terris nivis atque diræ
    Grandinis misit Pater." . .
† Dante, *Inferno*, cant. 6.

where I, unworthy commentator, have
seen it rain for fifty days, as if in
elucidation of this line alone. The
other Peninsula is not more favored
by heaven. The chancellor Ayala, a
learned man and one of high rank,
when lamenting the climate of Navarre,
is thus answered by the Castilian poet
Ferrus: "Would Hannibal ever have
conquered Spain had he dreaded the
snow and hail? and had the famous
Cid been afraid of showers, would be
have vanquished so many nobles and
kings?"* As for me, I should never
have aroused the ancient dead of Burgos had I not resolved to brave the
tempests unchained to defend their

---

* *Cancionero de Baena.*

solitude. It is true, I have seen the royal city under a veil, but a veil of rain is little favorable to illusions. Happily, however, if the age of heroes has left only walls and souvenirs, that of kings has bequeathed to posterity grander and more striking monuments.

When royalty established itself within the warlike enclosure of Diego Porcellos it assuredly brought grandeur, though not liberty, and Burgos grew in strength and fortune with this predestined monarchy, which, springing from the ravines of the Asturias, soon reached the banks of the Tagus, then the Guadalquivir, and finally the ocean. The noble city assumed the titles of Caput Castellae,

Madre de Reyes, y Restauradora de Reinos. Her coat of arms, which she bears even now, was the demi-figure of a crowned king upon a red ground, and surrounded by sixteen golden castles arranged in the shape of a St. Andrew's cross. At the cortes her deputies were on the king's right hand, those of Leon on the left, and when Toledo claimed the first rank she did not succeed in dispossessing Burgos, and her representatives had to content themselves with a position facing the throne.

The remains of the royal castle occupy, the summit of a hill which overlooks the city—a sombre, gloomy pile, and comparable to the Tower of London in point of bloodshed—for this was the scene of those fratricidal struggles so long the crime of Spain before God, her opprobrium before Christianity, and her weakness before infidels. Here Alfonso the Wise put to death his brother Don Fadrico, and Sancho the Brave, his brother Don Juan. These same walls witnessed the orgies and furies of Peter the Cruel, and in a more humane age, under Charles V., the public liberties here found a grave with the last chiefs of the commoners. From the heights of this citadel the kings held in check the aristocracy of ricos hombres, a military establishment connected with the seignorial houses of the Calle San Juan, Calle San Lorenzo, Calle d'Avellanos. Several of these edifices, renovated, it is true, in the fifteenth century, exteriorly remind one of dungeons, though in reality they are palaces, with hand-some courts ornamented with porticoes and colonnades. The dwelling of the constable Hernandez de Velasco sti l rears aloft its formidable façade, which looks as if built to sustain sieges. The collar of the Teutonic order, in deep relief, surrounds the entrance. But once through the menacing door and the patio opens before you, en-closed by elegant galleries and crown-ed with great terraces, whose open balustrades seem designed by a Flor-entine pencil. Add to this a profu-sion of drapery and flowers, the orches-tras and magnificently attired groups of people, everything that breathes of life, activity, and grace, and you will readily believe that this house was built for pleasure and festivals.

But to the honor of Castilian royalty and nobility, be it said, they spent less upon their own dwellings than upon the house of God. Accustomed to pass their lives in the camp, or on the battle-field, what need had they of magnificent arches or gilded panels? These luxuries they reserved for their Master's house, or the monasteries which sheltered their widows and daughters. Hence the numberless sanctuaries and religious establish-ments adorning Burgos: St. Esteban, a fine Gothic structure, decorated with the most beautiful caprices of the Renaissance; St. Gil, and its arched

chapels; St. Nicholas, and its altar-
piece, where, in sculptured stone, one
reads the legend of the saint. Every-
where do we see altars, mausoleums,
pious images, attesting the faith of
these proud families, who, though
wrathful and violent indeed, were not
insensible to the voices of religion and
repentance. The piety of the kings
has left a memento in those two grand
foundations, which are an embodiment,
as it were, of three hundred years of
history—the Abbey of Las Huelgas
and the Chartreuse of Miraflores.

To the southwest of Burgos, and
upon the left bank of the Arlanzon,
at the end of a few green lanes which
relieve the nakedness of the surrounding fields, arises a monastic fortress

enclosed by a double girdle of battlements. Its religious and feudal belfry
surmounted by a cross, but adorned
with machicolation, commands the plain.
Beneath this belfry is descried the side-
entrance to the church; and from one
side of the church an arched door
opens upon a vast court, at the further
end of which five gratings announce
the cloister of Santa Maria la Real de
las Huelgas. doubly celebrated, both
on account of the souvenirs connected
with its origin, and also because nowhere else in Christendom was so
great. ecclesiastical power ever wielded
by a woman. *

* I have consulted upon this subject the excellent memoir of M. the Abbé Calvos, one
of the chaplains of the house. M. the Abbé

Popular tradition, which is frequently capricious, and often maltreats its favorites, has cast a stain upon the life of Alphonso VIII., surnamed the Noble and the Good. "He became enamored of a Jewess," says the ballad. "Belle," (beautiful) "was her name, and one truly expressive of her appearance. For her he forsook the queen; with her he lived seven years." His nobles, touched by the queen's injuries, put her rival to death; and an angel appearing to the king, threatened him with eternal punishment. Shortly after, all the gorges of the Sierra Morena vomited forth torrents of infidels upon

Larran has also published an interesting notice upon the same subject, in the *Archæological Annals* of M. Didron.

Castile, and the Christian army was defeated at Alarcos, 1195. Tradition relates that Alphonso, repenting at last, founded the monastery of Las Huel-gas, and seventeen years after this God rewarded him by the victory of Tolosa de las Navas, in the year A.D. 1212. It was here the kings of Cas-tile, Aragon, and Navarre united their arms, whilst the whole Christian world, at the voice of the Sovereign Pon-tiff, had recourse to prayer. Heaven interposed in their behalf. A stranger, who was supposed to have been an angel, guided the Christians by paths unknown to the enemy, and a lumin-ous cross appeared in the air as the bishops exhorted the soldiers. Two hundred thousand unbelievers bit the dust. Meanwhile their chief, the Emii Amsir, whom the Spaniards called Miramolin, kept close in his tent, seated upon a shield and enveloped in a black mantle, one hand upon his scimiter, the other upon a gold and jewelled casket, containing the Alcoran. Here he remained, impassible apparently, giving no orders, and without uttering other words than "God alone is true, and Satan false!" At this moment an Arab brings him a mare. Mounting it, and the Arab his horse, they escape unnoticed amidst the mighty host seeking refuge in flight. Leaving behind his banner and casket of the Alcoran, these rich spoils were given to the monastery of Las Huelgas. The casket disappeared in

1808, but the banner remains, and is
exhibited every year on the anniversary of the battle. On this anniversary—the 16th of July, which has
become a festival of the Church, under
the title of the Triumph of the Cross—
the tomb of Alphouso VIII. is decorated
with lights and flowers. Truth and
falsehood are mingled in these accounts.
The episode of the beautiful Jewess
has no foundation, neither was the
monastery erected to appease the wrath
of Heaven, so visibly declared in the
defeat at Alarcos, for its erection pre-
ceded the latter event by several years.
About the year 1180, Alphonso VIII.,
at the instance of his wife, Queen
Eleanor, and his daughters, Urracha
and Berengera, resolved to found an

abbey of women on the very spot
where then stood one of the royal resi-
dences, a castle less sombre in appearance than that of Burgos, and styled
Las Huelgas del Re – the king's leisure. In 1187 he gave the dwelling
and surroundings to Doña Maria Sol,
a Cistercian religious, and her companions. At last, by a rescript of
December 14, 1199, furnished with
the royal seal, and bearing the signa-
tures of ten bishops and eleven ricos
hombres, the donation. with the addition of the following promise, was
ratified, and placed in the hands of
Guy, Abbé of Citeaux : " Moreover,
we promise the said abbé that we and
our descendants, if they carry out our
counsels and commands, will be buried

in the said monastery of Santa Maria
la Real, and should it happen that,
living, we wished to embrace the religious state, we promise to receive the
habit of Citeaux and no other."

The successors of Alphonso VIII. finished his work. Alphonso X. restricted
the number of religious to a hundred,
all nobles. The concessions of kings, the
constitutions of popes and the abbés of
Citeaux, assured to Santa Maria de las
Huelgas that wealth, that canonical and
civil jurisdiction, which gave its abbesses
the first rank among the Castilian
nobility and the Christian hierarchy.

As to civil jurisdiction, the ladies of
Las Huelgas had the seigniory of fifty-
one hamlets and villages, with the
*imperium merum et mixtum;* the cog-

nizance of civil and criminal cases, the
nomination of magistrates, clerks, col-
lectors. The officers of justice of Burgos could not penetrate here with
uplifted rods, they were either lowered
on entering or left at the door; whilst,
or the other hand, the abbess had a
judge at Burgos for the conservation
of her rights over the grain and vege-
tables sold in market. St. Ferdinand
added to this the whole of the crown
taxes upon the Arlanzon's waters at
night and one-half of the day's returns.

As to canonical powers, the abbey
of Las Huelgas under no episcopal authority (*nullius diœcesis*), mother house
of the Cistercian convents throughout
Castile and Leon, exercised a legiti-
mate jurisdiction over the monasteries,

churches, hermitages of its order---a jurisdiction derogatory to that of the archbishops and diocesan bishops. The abbess by her delegates had the first knowledge of all beneficiary cases, the right of filling curacies and chaplaincies, that of examining, approving, and conceeling the necessary titles to celebrate, preach, confess, and have the charge of souls. She was acquainted with the violations of enclosure, the immunities of churches, translations of convents, erection of confraternities, and she could likewise tender letters of recommendation for holy orders.

No doubt the Abbesses of Chelles and Fontevrault more than once waved their monastic coat of arms

beside the lilies of France; they num-
bered among their followers a host of
barons and chevaliers; they sent deputies to the States-General, and their
quota to the royal standard. Germany,
too. could boast of her superb religious, in whose presence the Emperor
arose, and who occupied a seat in the
Diet. But the canonists nowhere
mention another example of such ex-
orbitant power as that exercised by the
ladies of Las Huelgas in the face of
that powerful metropolitan the Archbishop of Burgos, who dwelt at the
opposite end of the bridge. It was
the policy of the kings to aggrandize
a house which they regarded as their
own, where. with their families, they
would repose in death; where the

princesses of their blood could ever find a retreat, whether they took the veil or retired thither for only a few years of cloistral repose. Here we see six Infants of Castile, three of Aragon, one of Navarre, one of Portugal, one of Austria. On their side the popes could not refuse these unprecedented honors to the daughters of a royal race, who had sustained against the infidels a crusade of eight hundred years. In no country more than Spain did women need that protection which springs from respect, for in no country did they lack more the protection of the sword, the family rampart; nowhere were they condemned to a longer solitude, a more certain widowhood, whilst endless warfare claimed husbands, brothers, sons. In the Middle Ages, woman was honored throughout Christendom; in France and Italy, warriors and poets were at her service; in Castile, religious and priests ranged themselved under her laws.*

You will probably reproach me with having stopped to talk before the abbey grating, instead of penetrating

---

* We must read, in the *Memoir of the Abbé Calvo*, the royal ordinance of January 22, 1728, by which King Philip V. confirms the privileges of the abbey of Las Huelgas, referring to the concessions of Popes Clement III., Gregory IX., Innocent IV., Innocent VIII., Leo X., Pius V., Urban VIII. It is true, the texts of these concessions are not given, whilst at the same time we see the royal abbey pleading against the archbishops to be delivered from the consultations of doctors, which proves that its rights could be contested.

these cloisters, whose marvellous beauties you have heard described. Doubt-
less, you are longing to see the cloisters especially and their Roman arcades, relics of the palace of Alphonso
VIII., the doors with their Moresque
decorations, the grand arched cloister.
Here every epoch of Spanish architecture has left its trace; but you
must believe this, if you please, upon
the word of the archæologists, for the
grates open not to us; an immutable
law keeps them for ever shut against
all save the King and Queen of Spain.
When one of these sovereigns visits
the house, the train of attendants is
also permitted to enter. Then the
whole city numbers itself upon the
list of royal attendants and it is thus

some fortunate stranger, led hither by his star, finds the opportunity of sketching these graceful lines, these capricious ornaments, which are now your envy and despair.

The church, however, remains to us, though even here the same severe law robs us of half its beauties. The lateral door opens upon an *atrium*, called the *nave de los caballeros*. There, under bare or rudely-sculptured tombs, the old Castilian chevaliers guard their dead kings, like good servants reposing at their masters' doors. Let us enter the basilica, forgetting the modern decorations which deface the sanctuary, and regardless of the grate, which prevents us from visiting but not from viewing the choir of the religious, the ten arcades of the grand nave, and the tombs. We find that the genius of St. Ferdinand—that brave and pious monarch, the captor of cities and founder of so many churches — still breathes in every line of this beautiful edifice, which his piety rebuilt. The plan is that of a Latin cross. Before the completion of its cathedral, Burgos contained no structure more grave and majestic than this, where the Byzantine severity serves, we might say, as a stem for the first bloom of Gothic architecture. We perceive that the sovereigns of the thirteenth age transformed the royal church, the basilica of their festivals and triumphs, into a place of sepulture—in other words, they made it the St. Denis of old Castile.

For five hundred years the successors of Alphonso VIII. scarcely knew that leisure whence springs the splendor of a reign and a capital's prosperity. We see them forcing the gates of Seville, Xeres, Gibraltar, or shut up in Toledo, in order to watch more closely the enemy's movements. But most always at Burgos, and at St. Mary's of Las Huelgas, do they seek their coronation, their nuptial benediction, and the only peace they ever found—that of the grave. Here St. Ferdinand was knighted; the bishop Maurice blessed the arms, and Ferdinand himself took the sword from the altar, but he would have it girded on by no hands save those of his mother. Here Alphonso XI., Henry II., and

Juan I. celebrated their coronation,
and to end where all earthly grandeur
ends, here, too, in the centre of the
choir, is the tomb of Alphonso VIII
and his wife Eleanor, whilst the grand
and side naves contain the remains of
Alphonso VII., Sancho III., Henri I.,
Alphonso X.—of five queens, eleven
princes, and eighteen princesses. The
mausoleums are for the most part
very simple, usually supported by lions,
and ornamented only with arabesques
and statuettes arranged in the niches.
Yet this long line of kings and
princes still consoles the widowhood
of the old city of Burgos, by recalling
the days when her palaces were not,
as now, silent and abandoned.*

* Upon the architecture of the church of Las

The founder of Las Huelgas not only provided for the repose of his descendants, but, with touching kindness, he also established a resting-place for poor travellers and pilgrims, who, from all parts of Christendom, repaired to St. James of Compostello. Near the royal abbey, and under its jurisdiction, is the Hospital del Rey, where thirteen men and several of the other sex (all religious) serve the pilgrims in the name of their abbess. To honor their ministry, they wear the habit of Calatrava, and are entitled *comendadores* and *comendaoras*. The

Huelgas, we must consult a learned article of M Didron in the *Archæological Annals* of 1849. Circumstances have prevented my examining this as well as many other authorities.

hospital contained a hundred and twelve beds, and fed, in addition four hundred persons. Revolutions have destroyed this stewardship of ancient hospitality, and restorations have disfigured the architecture. Yet who could forbear stopping at this elegant gate (*puerta de los Romeros*), where the fatigued traveller's first glance descries the images of his celestial protectors — St. James majestically seated in a niche, and, above, the Archangel Michael, crushing under foot the dragon. Tradition states that the porter to this entrance was the blessed St. Amaro. He came from France, says this legend, and, having fulfilled his vow at Compostello, remained to spend his days in

the service of the pilgrims, washing
their feet, dressing their wounds, has-
tening to meet the most fatigued and
carrying them on his shoulders. Profound obscurity enveloped the life of
this just man, but the night of his
death a brilliant light enveloped the
Hospital del Rey. The people of
Burgos ran to the spot, believing the
house in flames, but found that it was
a token from heaven by which God
wished to honor and reveal the
hidden virtues of his servant. The
Church erected altars to St. Amaro,
and the people still read with devotion the legend of his life. Here we
must stop to dwell a moment upon
one of the characteristics of Catholic
Spain—charity beside grandeur. The

Cid wreaks vengeance upon the Saracen, but the leper sits at his table and
reposes upon his bed. The abbesses
of Las Huelgas reign behind their
convent grates, which are opened only
to crowned heads, but the gates of
their hospital are never shut against
the poor.*

Santa Maria de las Huelgas guards
Burgos on the west, whilst the Carthusian convent of Miraflores protects
it on the east. It was thus the cities
of the Middle Ages loved to be en-
compassed by these monastic camps,
where watched the servants of God,
sentinels of prayer and penitence.

> " Nisi Dominus custodierit civitatem
> Frustra vigilat qui custodit eam."

* *Apuntes sobre Burgos.*

The Carthusian monastery is situated upon a hill commanding the country, but whence one descries only monotonous fields of wheat and barley. How this graceful name of Miraflores deceives us, for we see no flowers but the pale mallows, scattered by autumnal winds! For a long time have I been forced to renounce the Castile of my dreams, abounding with luxuriant gardens, purple pomegranates, citrons bending under the weight of their golden fruit, whilst the fragrant white jasmine clambered up the balcony lattices, and, I need scarcely add, the palm, crowning with its triumphal branches this rich vegetation of the south.

As the road from Burgos to the

chartreuse is long, I shall profit by
the opportunity to entertain you with
a short account of King Juan II., not,
however, without a show of reason, since
we are going to visit places redolent
of his memory, and since the poetic
splendor of his reign was reflected in
the works of art we are about to see.
You will begin to suspect me of introducing here, under the cover of a
journey, detached chapters of a history of Spanish literature. Heaven
shield me from this excess of perfidy!
But how shall I deny that for me the
greatest attraction, the magic, of this
journey consists in transporting me,
not only to other climes, but to distant ages? To my eyes, these grand
historic countries would be but la

mentable cemeteries, could I not, in passing through, awaken to life the generations who once peopled them. And what better mode of reanimation than that of giving them speech, especially the words of their own poets, which express, with the utmost *naïveté,* vigor, and brilliancy, the thoughts of all?

We are now in the middle of the fifteenth century. We hear no longer those warlike poets whom St. Ferdinand led to battle, or those recitations of exploits which the ancient chevaliers had sung at their tables. Gradually, the heroic ballad, with its simplicity of style, its irregularity of versification, loses popularity, except with an ignorant auditory of peasants and soldiers collected around some blind singer. Another style of poetry is now the pastime of a rich, refined, and exacting society. The Provençal troubadours frequent the courts of Aragon and Castile. Here they at first find admirers, then disciples. The *ricos hombres* strive to compose *sirventes* and *canzons*. The consistory of Gay Science, at Barcelona, displays a concourse which rivals the floral games of Toulouse. Meanwhile, the Spaniards have crossed the sea, and returned from their conquest of Sicily and Naples, their ears still attuned to the songs of the Italian muse, their souls inflamed with that passion of antiquity which animated the Roman and Florentine savants. In one year, 1428, appeared two translations of the *Divina Commedia*, one in Catalonian and one in Castilian. Others imitated Petrarch, or translated Titus Livius. But the refined learning of Provence and Italy could be acclimatized only under the shadow of the palace. It needed the protection of a beneficent, cultivated prince, clever and witty rather than great. This prince, this Medicis of the Castilian revival, was Juan II.

History has already passed sentence upon the prince, who occupied the throne forty-eight years without reigning, the slave of his favorite, Alvaro de Luna—afterwards of the faction which made him sign that same favorite's death-warrant—dying at last fully impressed with a knowledge of his own

weakness and inutility, and condemn-
ing himself in these his dying words:
"Would to God I had been born the
son of a mechanic, and had lived a
monk at the convent of Abrojo!"
Yet this man, incapable of governing
wills or suppressing intrigues and in-
surrections, enjoyed a pacific reign in
the world of arts and letters. A great
painter of times and manners—Fernan
Perez de Gusman—thus depicts the
literary character of King Juan II.:
"He understood men, and readily dis-
tinguished those who conversed intelli-
gently and agreeably. He appreciated
their society, and treasured their words.
He understood and spoke Latin. He
read well, and was fond of books. He
relished true poetry, and with equal

facility discerned ill-made verse. He
took great pleasure in lively, witty
conversations, in which he was by no
means incapable of bearing his part.
Versed in music, he sang and played.'
He himself did not disdain to com
pose, and he was sufficiently successfu.
to chant in light rhymes the power c
love and cruelty of woman. How
ever, his greatest merit, lay in en-
couraging and consequently multiplying
poetic talent, and thus forming around
his throne a Pleiad of splendor. Upon
its blood-stained steps one hears only
songs and poems of every metre. The
grand constable Alvaro de Luna dic-
tates couplets whilst meditating the
designs that lead him to the scaffold.
The Marquis of Villena sketches a

poetic art. The Marquis of Santillane
counts, with his iron - manacled hand,
the syllabled cadences of his sonnets
The commander Calavera proposes a
poetical contest upon a given subject—
"The reconciliation of Providence with
man's free will" — and seven poets
answer the summons, among them a
monk and a Mahometan. A fruitful
disorder, a beneficent equality, con-
found all rank and distinction when
one applies his hand to verse-making.
Bishops and state officials carry on
a correspondence with Montoro, the
dealer in old clothes; Juan, the har-
ness-maker; Mondragon, the groom;
Juan of Valladolid, son of an execu-
tioner, and a hotel servant. The demon of verse possesses the Spanish

nation, and the school to which it gives birth, though one of necessity, is laborious, elegant, witty, yet cold and empty.*

The fifteenth century is also a tragic age. The Christians of Spain waged war among themselves, whilst from all the towers of Granada the infidels kept unceasing watch, awaiting but a favorable moment to cast themselves upon the divided, exhausted kingdom. Yet the *Cancionero de Baena*, containing the collected productions of fifty authors, scarcely betrays a trace of

---

* Ticknor, *History of Spanish Literature*, vol. i. See also M. Pidal's learned introduction to the *Cancionero de Baena*, and an article of M. Leopoldo de Cueto, *Revue des Deux Mondes*, May 15, 1853.

either these civil or holy wars, in which
the poets and their Macænases risked
their lives. The more seriously dis-
posed cultivated a learned style of
poetry, after the example of Dante,
henceforth established master of the
Castilian Parnassus.* These seldom
failed to wander in some forest, where
accidentally meeting a mysterious per-
sonage who became their guide, they
were conducted into a place where
they discovered the harmony between
divine and human things. However,
one does not often approach great
models without deriving some benefit
therefrom, Juan de Mena owes to his
imitation of the *Divina Commedia* an

* *Cancionero de Baena*, page 261: "Requesta de
Alfonso Alvares contra Ferrant Manuel."

elevation of style that places him immensely above his contemporaries. By far the greater number followed in the train of the Provençal poets, preferring that light and gallant style of poetry which enkindles so many flames and sharpens so many arrows, but without costing its votaries life. If the too sensitive Macias fell a victim to his passion, his was a solitary case, which became the admiration of all posterity, and the happy versificators of the court of Juan II. rhymed peacefully upon the *Mandates of Love*, the *Pleas of Love*, the *Regrets of Love*, the *Prison of Love*, and even the *Hell of Love*. Leaving aside the national epics, the productions of the period are miserable, and this art of imitation seems only the art of decadence, though here, as is often the case elsewhere, it is a decadence concealing a progress. The poetic worship of women added gentleness and delicacy to Castilian valor. It permeated, if not all souls, at least the language and manners with those lofty sentiments, making Spanish society a school of honor and courtesy, and which, crossing the Pyrenees with Anne of Austria, gave the finishing polish to French society. But in these efforts of the fifteenth century to reproduce the rhythms of Italy and Provence, and even in this excessive chiselling of verse and stanza, we see accomplished its especial though involuntary work, which was to transform and refine the rude language of the Cid

This poetry, which remained content with faulty measure and facile assonance, was to become flexible and capable of the utmost precision and most exquisite melody, but it must pass through a long novitiate ere reaching the moment when Calderon, recovering the inspiration of Christianity's palmy days, would crown it with the prestige of a brilliant, musical language, untranslatable for us, but ineffably enchanting to the Spanish ear. This rapid glance at the literary aspect of the court of Juan II. was necessary as a preparation for an appreciative visit to his tomb. The Castilian revival can now unfold to our gaze its marvels of sculpture—we know whence sprang the breeze that opened these blossoms of marble and stone.

Whilst talking, we have just passed through the arched gateway which marked the limits of the royal park at Miraflores. Juan II., carrying out a vow made by his father Henry III., donated to the monks the park and pavilion where the kings were accustomed to rest after the chase; and finally, sufficient money to erect a monastery, beneath whose shadow he wished to sleep in death. On the Feast of Pentecost, 1442, the community was established; and to the joyful sounds of a hunting rendezvous succeeded the silence of St. Bruno's rule. But Juan II. dying before the completion of the new monastery, that work was reserved for the great Isabella, the same who wielded such an influence over Spain and the whole world. Two German architects, Jean and Simon of Cologne, and two Spanish, Garcia Fernandez Martienzo and Diego de Mondieta, built the august and elegant church. Before the vaults were closed, Isabella had provided, for the sepulture of her father. Repairing to Miraflores, in 1483, she had his coffin, which had been temporarily deposited in one of the vaults, brought forth and opened, that she might see the body and kiss its feet. Soon after she commissioned the sculptor Gil de Siloe to execute the two mausoleums of Juan II. and Isabella of Portugal, his second wife, and Don Alphonso, their son. The designs were submitted to her, and the sculptor having applied his chisel to the marble in 1489, pursued the work so vigorously that in less than five months both tombs were finished. *

The church of Miraflores, then, is an immense reliquary, in which the piety of Isabella has enshrined the remains of her father, mother, and the young brother whose premature death placed the crown upon her brow. Exteriorly, the church resembles a catafalque—no steeple, no transept in front, no ornament save the heraldic emblazonry one sees upon the mortuary wrappings

* Arias, *Apuntes Historicos sobre la Cartuja de Miraflores.* I have profited much by this excellent work.

of a king; the roof rounded like a coffin lid, the crucifix at the entrance, and ranged all around forty small spires of three different heights, like the three rows of candelabras around a bier. But enter this abode of death and you will find there all the typified splendor of a Christian hope. The mind disengages itself from earth, and rises heavenward with these aspiring arches. The promise of immortality beams forth from these fourteen stone fasces, starting from the angels of the apsis, and whose inlerlacing nerves hang in graceful festoons above the sanctuary. Seventeen stained glass windows admit a light, mysterious and clear as that of faith. The united efforts of sun and rain have tarnished their beauties, but they h.ve not effaced the life of our Saviour, which forms the subject, and which for us is truly the only light capable of dissipating the shades of death.

A merchant of Burgos having been charged with a commission in Flanders for the windows of Miraflores, presumed to make a present of one stamped with his own arms. When Isabella was informed of this unknown emblazonry, taking a sword from one of the gentlemen in her train, she broke the glass to pieces. "In this house," said she, "I wish no arms but those of my Father." She herself, who had erected these walls and tombs, nowhere inscribed her name, though truly everything proclaims it. Crown-

ng the altar-piece of gilded wood,
appears Christ on the cross, not accompanied by the pope and emperor,
as he is frequently represented in the
Middle Ages, but sustained on one
side by a pope wearing the tiara and
on the other by a crowned queen.
And how can we forget that, at the
very time when Isabella was occu·
pied with this work, Christopher Columbus returned from that New World
to which he had opened his way,
made his triumphal entry into Burgos,
leading in his train a number of sav-
iges, crowned with glittering plumes,
and bringing as offerings to the
queen a diadem, a chain, bracelets, and
ingots of the purest gold? These
riches she consecrated to the service of

God, and thus the altar-piece of Miraflores was adorned with the first-fruits
of America.*

Were the place less rich in marvels,
we might stop at the monks' stalls or
the dais which surmounts the prior's
seat. But I have no longer a thought
for anything save the monument aris-
ing before the altar, from the centre of the choir. The two statues
of Juan II. and Isabella of Portugal,
recline upon an octagon base. The
heads are beautiful, the attitudes noble
and calm, the costumes magnificent.
The king appears such as his contemporaries have represented him — " tall

* Arias, *Apuntes*, pp 71, 77, 78. This refers to
the second return of Christophe. Columbus from
America, in 1496 ,

and finely formed, of an aspect truly
royal, his limbs, hands, and feet perfect. Moreover, he was frank and gracious, devout and valiant, a great
scholar, and very prepossessing in appearance." But on scanning these
somewhat effeminate features more
closely, we discover likewise the timid
prince, the sport of those factions
afflicting his reign, and which are fitly
typified in the two lions struggling at
his feet. The queen reposes beside
him, but inclining slightly to the opposite side, as if from bashfulness. Her
eyes are cast upon a book she holds
in her hands, and in whose pages she
seeks forgetfulness of pomps and royal
cares. At her feet play together a lion,
a dog, and a child; thus opposing to

the remembrance of civil discord an image of domestic peace. Around these two sovereigns, laid low in death, the four Evangelists are seated upon thrones, whose stability knows not the blight of time. The artist has thrown into the expression of these heads a truly Spanish pride, which proclaims unrelenting defiance to the Mussulman and Jew. Between these figures, and at the eight angles of the sub-base, arise angels on outspread wing. The sub-base itself is a world of statues and statuettes, seated or standing, prominent or buried in niches, or veiled under leaves. Sixteen personages oc-cupy the principal place — on the king's side, eight of the just men of the Old Testament; on the queen's, the theological and cardinal virtues, and the Virgin holding the dead Christ upon her knees, as if reminding us that royal souls are not exempt from sorrow. All around, above, beneath, are doctors meditating, enveloped in their mantles; cowled monks praying, and a shepherd caressing his sheep. We might justly say that Art had sought throughout creation, from the angels and heavenly virtues to the beasts of the earth, for whatever was strongest and purest, holiest and most intelligent, to sustain the weight of this king and queen, who were Christians, but sinners likewise.

"Si iniquitates observaveris, Domine,
Domine, quis sustinebit?"

Their daughter would not leave

them solitary in the tomb. She surrounded them with all these people of
stone, seemingly interceding for them
before the Lord

Notwithstanding the beauties of so
great a work, good judges prefer the
Infant's tomb. The days of this youth
were short and evil. In the time of
his elder brother, Henry IV., the Im-
potent, whose reign separated those of
Juan II. and Isabella, Alphonso fell
into the hands of the insurgents. The
chief of the Castilian nobles, for
the gratification of his own ambitious
schemes, scrupled not to lay violent
hands upon a child, and engage him
in a fratricidal struggle; and it is this
child who figures in the memorable
scene thus described by a contempo-

rary ;* " In the plain near Avila was erected a scaffold, and upon it placed an effigy of King Henry, seated on a throne and dressed in mourning. After the crowd had listened to a long list of grievances against the king, he was declared unworthy of re'gning. Then the Archbishop of Toledo approached the effigy, and took off its crown. He was declared unworthy of governing, and the Count of Benavente snatched away the sceptre. Fi-

* *Henriqued el Castillo,* translation of M. Ternaux. Calderon has transferred this scene to his beautiful tragedy, *El Principe dé Fez,* where the Mussulman prince, on the eve of becoming a Christian, is persecuted by the demon, and sees, in a dream, his people rise up against him, his effigy hurled from the throne, and his young son crowned in his stead.

nally, the figure was ignominiously hurl
ed from the throne, and the Infant
Don Alphonso elevated to the vacancy,
whilst the royal standard was unfurled
and with one voice the people cried
out: 'Castile, Castile for King Al
phonso!'" But the young Alphonso's
reign was short. Death claimed its
own; and the honors of this false royalty reflect less glory upon his memory
than the monument erected by Isabella's affection and the chisel of Gil
de Siloe. The base of the tomb con
sists of the escutcheon of Castile and
Leon, flanked by two mail-clad warriors, resting upon their lances, their
proud, defiant countenances betokening
at once those mighty vassals who
were less the guardians of the crown

tnan its peril and incessant dread.
Above this is the Infant Don Alphonso, kneeling upon cushions. He
is arrayed in a rich mantle, the chape-
ron upon his shoulders, and before him,
on an ottoman, an open book. A
sculptured garland floats above him,
like a curtain which is about to fall.
The arcade enclosing this scene terminates by an image of Our Lady with
the Infant Jesus. On two sides of
the monument arise two splendid pyra-
mids, in ornamental tracery, and peopled with groups of small though per-
fectly-executed figures. But I should
never finish did I stop to describe the
capricious arabesques, the poetic epi-
sodes, which enrich this composition.
Among other charming pictures is that

of a youth stretching forth his hand
to pluck a bunch of grapes that seemed to have ripened especially for him;
but just as he does so, a squirrel,
more agile, darts down the lattice,
and devours them before his eyes.
Is not this an image of that child
born for the crown, which a premature destiny snatches from it? • Virgil,
in immortal verse, bewailed the short
years of the young Marcellus; the Castilian sculptor makes the cold marble
sigh for the young Alphonso. The
same moan arises from poem and
tomb.

"Ostendent terris hunc tantum fata, nec ultra
    Esse sinent."    .    .    .    .    .    .

And let no one accuse me of attributing meaning to the caprices of artists, and of introducing allusion and symbol, where they gave but freedom to their imagination and delicacy to their chisel. It would be unbecoming in us, who are their inferiors in this respect, to lend inspiration to the fifteenth · century and its artists, the most ingenious, subtle, and amorous that ever existed. When Juan de Mena could extend his allegorical poem to the length of three hundred octaves, why should not the sculptor adorn his subject with these emblems, which were understood and appreciated by all his contemporaries? The same taste, the same refinement, the same patience that softened and harmonized the language and interlaced rhymes,

awakened from the stone its scrolls,
its foliage and flowers. Here, too, as
in the province of letters, the Castilian
genius is founded upon that of the
stranger. Those Germans from Cologne, who came hither to build the
chartreuse, heirs of Gothic tradition,
taught the Spaniards how to translate
Christian theology into bas-reliefs and
statues. The monks and doctors on
the mausoleum of Juan II. bear a
striking resemblance to the mourners
of Our Lady of Brou, and the arabesques on the Infanta's tomb recall
the most beautiful fantasies of the
Italian sculptors. Thus the history
of poesy repeats itself in the history of
the arts, or, in other words, it is the
same poetic genius that guides the pen

and chisel. But in Spain the latter was at first more powerful than the pen, it did more than diffuse around it grace and elegance—it gave soul and thought. The Church of Miraflores alone—that funeral monument—contains more life than the *Cancionero de Baena*, and the Spanish revival had already found in the arts that spirit of beauty she still sought among letters. However, in descending a little from the time of King Juan II., I find the following memento of his reign in lines not unworthy of quotation, and which recall in a moment the splendor of that learned and frivolous court:

."What has become of King Don Juan? The Infantas of Aragon, where are they? What now remains of so much gallantry, so much contrivance, displayed in all their sports? The tilts and tourneys, the ornaments and embroidery, the crests, like the visions of a dream—what were all these things but verdure of the field?

"What has become of these noble ladies—their coiffures, their vestments, and perfumes? Where are now those fireside flames that shone upon so many happy faces? What has become of the troubadour's art and those harmonious instruments?—those dances and costly stuffs worked with gold and silver?

"The liberal largesses, the royal edifices filled with gold, the handsomely wrought plate, the crowns and reals of the treasury, the horses and rich ca parison of the king's attendants—where shall we go to seek them? What were they all but the dew upon the meadow?"*

With the reign of Juan II. ended the reign of grandeur for Burgos. Isabella several times visited the capital and her father's tomb, and Charles V. was seen there, but gradually the kings grew estranged from the old city, and never appeared at Miraflores except when passing by. The monks alone remained, guardian of the sepulchres and dispensers of a lordly hospitality, for the monastery was the abundant granary of the indigent, the resource in years of famine. Besides affording

---

* Jorge Manrique. Coplas a la muerte de su padre.

needful succor in great public calamities, the religious every day dined fifteen paupers, taken from the list of twenty honorable men and thirty-two students, who must prove their need and good character. But now, even the monks themselves—these last mandatories of the kings—have also disappeared. The younger members of the community have regained the icy solitude of the Alps, whence descended to Spain St. Bruno's rule, and three old men (seculars) are the sole occupants of these empty cloisters. The chant of Psalms which, night and day for three hundred years, was heard around these tombs, has ceased, and the monastery itself would be but a soulless body did not the God of Heaven daily descend upon the altar, for the repose of the dead who built, and the benefit of the living who have profaned it.

Before quitting the city of kings, I forgot to attend the royal spectacle of a bull-fight. But I am too well acquainted with my duties to omit this binding episode of a journey to Spain. Every year, at a certain period, the grand square of Burgos, with its porticoes and its even rows of windows, is transformed into an amphitheatre. Unfortunately for us, the festal times were over, and the lists were crossed only by women singing some joyous refrain, as, with jar gracefully poised on their heads, they wended their way to the fountain. Nevertheless, the combat must be described, even should I seek it elsewhere. Well, then, I have seen the black bull of Navarre rush madly forward with lowered horns, foaming and tearing the ground at his feet! I have seen the runners tantalize him with a drapery of bright colors waved before his eyes, and then at one bound disappear behind the palisade which encloses the arena. But the furious beast dashed after them, and when I believed them lost, pent up with him in this narrow gallery, they suddenly reappeared, calm and proud, at their posts in the arena. I could not help admiring these men, so becomingly arrayed in doublet and slashed small clothes, so strong and active, and so graceful in their movements, as to banish all thought of danger. But when, the combat waxing warm, a host of banderilleros tormented the intrepid animal, by planting between its horns the dart which brought forth jets of blood, or the rocket which enveloped it in fire—when, blinded and seeing its enemies no longer, the poor creature ran here and there, bellowing with pain and fury, and when at last a matador, in habit embroidered with gold or silver, grasping his sword and bending one knee to earth, asked permission to strike, then I must confess my sympathy was entirely for the bull, and I lacked courage to notice whether or not the blow was struck according to the rules, for, detesting such butchery, I abruptly left the amphitheatre whilst six mules, to the noise of trumpets

and the tumultuous applause of an ex
cited crowd, dragged away the bloody
body.

# V.

## THE CITY OF THE VIRGIN.

Burgos, November 20, 1852.

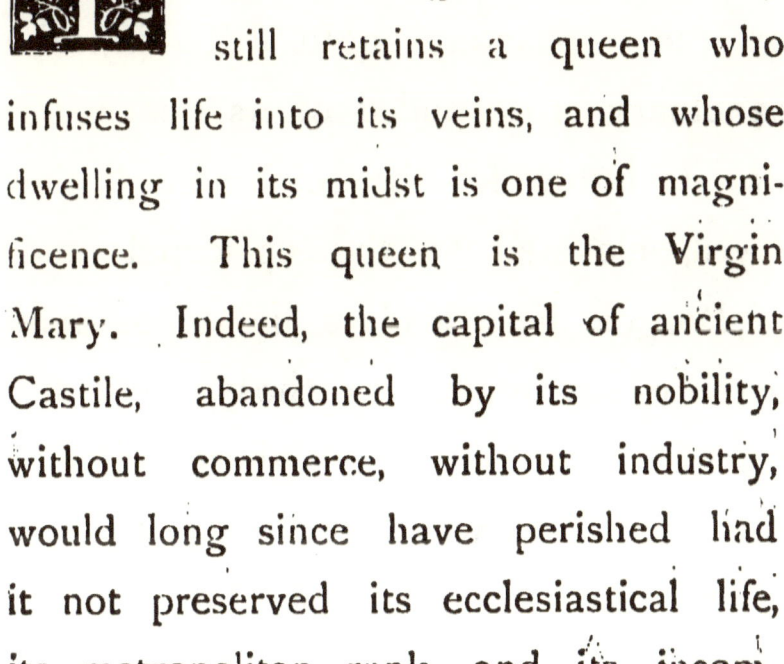

THOUGH its kings have de-
serted Burgos, the old city
still retains a queen who
infuses life into its veins, and whose
dwelling in its midst is one of magnificence. This queen is the Virgin
Mary. Indeed, the capital of ancient
Castile, abandoned by its nobility,
without commerce, without industry,
would long since have perished had
it not preserved its ecclesiastical life,
its metropolitan rank, and its incom-

parable cathedral. The power of this
archbishopric, and the religious estab-
lishments springing up beneath its
shadow, brought together a large and
intelligent body of the clergy. So
many churches, so many convents, ne
cessarily attracted a number of clerks,
artisans, and even the poor, too well
assured, perhaps, of always finding soup
at the monastery gate. To-day the
sanctuary is despoiled of its riches, but
not its lights, for the celebrated Father
Cyril, elevated to the episcopal chair
of Burgos, here leads a life of peaceful
activity, surrounded by those good and
learned men from the highest ranks of
the hierarchy, who have so justly sustained the reputation of the Spanish
clergy. Among them, I may mention

the venerable M. Orteaga y Ercilla, archdean of the Chapter (*arcideano*), a profound theologian and a promoter of every good work, animating, by example and co-operation, an innumerable throng of young and pious laymen. With what regret we spoke of the learned and judicious Balmés, so early snatched away, not only from his country, but from the church and Christian philosophy! What hopes we built upon that less staunch, but generous and brilliant spirit, upon those bold thoughts and eloquent words of Donoso Cortés, little dreaming that this second star of the Spanish firmament was so soon to be extinguished! Yet I never fear eternal shades for a Catholic country, where science is ranked among the gifts of the Holy Ghost, and its cultivation one of the duties of a priest. St. Jerome's College at Burgos teaches the ancient and oriental languages. There are two good primary schools for boys, and it is not without pleasure I see so many rustics buying romances and legends, the literature of a simple people, I must admit, but still of a people who can at least read.

I have said that the Virgin Mary is the queen of this people. And in reality, during the Middle Ages, the estate of an episcopal church always belonged to the titular saint. He was considered guardian of the ecclesiastical patrimony, in his name were made out the legacies and donations, in his

hands lay the chastisement of profa-
nations. Burgos, then, was Our Lady's
domain, and here is the legend : Whilst
evangelizing Spain, the Apostle St.
James stops at Saragossa, where he
converts eight pagans. Fatigued, perhaps, with the discussion, he falls asleep
at the foot of a pillar; when, surrounded by angels, the Blessed Virgin
suddenly appears, and addressing herself to the apostle, inspires him with
renewed ardor. Resuming his travels,
he penetrates to the very heart of old
Castile, and erects at Auca an episcopal see, in which he is succeeded
by his disciple Indalecius But Auca
and its bishopric, swept away by a
Mussulman invasion, disappeared until
1075, when Bishop Ximeno removed

to Burgos his predecessors' bones and
the Virgin's antique image, before which
they had prayed. The first edifice was
a poor and humble oratory. But when
the glorious days of St. Ferdinand had
come, this great king, who erected the
cathedrals of Toledo, Osma, Tuy, and
Orense, cheerfully gave up his palace
to Bishop Maurice that it might make
way for Our Lady of Burgos. Maurice, who planned the church, laid the
first stone on the 20th of July, 1221.
The proportions he wished spacious
and imposing, such as were fitting the
capital of a victorious people, but the
very grandeur of the design prevented
his living to see its accomplishment.
The Spaniards, who are never prompt
in execution, who took eight hundred

years to reconquer their country, were
more than two centuries finishing their
cathedral. It seems even that the Virgin, as if meaning to reprove the tar-
diness of these old Christians, selected
from a despised race the man who
was to finish St. Ferdinand's work—
this was the Bishop Alonso, a con-
verted Jew of a strict Pharisee family,
yet which gloried in being descendants of the same line as Mary the
Mother of Jesus. Baptized in youth,
with his father and four brothers, he
received holy orders, became Bishop of
Burgos, and one of the lights of the
Spanish Church, which he represented
nobly at the Council of Bâle. Returning from the borders of the Rhine,
he brought with him Jean of Cologne

who, in 1442, resuming the interrupted work, elevated the façade, and flanked it with the two towers.*

After visiting the walls of Diego Porcellos, the remains of the royal castle, and the arch of Fernan Gonzalez, the first sight that strikes us on leaving these sad, deserted quarters is the façade of the cathedral with its two arrowy steeples, and gazing on this edifice, which never grows old, we bless God for having placed upon earth a power more durable than that of heroes and kings.

The Cathedral of Burgos has truly the appearance of a new edifice. Though not without majesty, its chief

* Dom Pedro Orcajo, *Historia de la Catedral de Burgos.* Pons, *Viage.*

points are elegance and grace. I can not, however, include here the first steps of the façade or the principal entrance, disfigured by modern vandalism. But above this degraded sub-base arises the Gothic arch, and still higher, a rich gallery displays under its arcades eight statues of kings ranged like a guard of honor; then, two long arched windows, and the front of the edifice terminates in a marvellously wrought railing, the design forming this inscription: " *Tota pulchra es et decora.*" The towers that flank the two sides attain each a height of three hundred feet, and though unparalleled in the delicacy of their net-work, they defy all the storms of Castile. The embroidery of stone surrounding them forms on one side the words *Agnus Dei;* on the other, *Pax vobis*, and these peaceful proclamations in an age of violence were no less miraculous than the two arrowy spires, firm and unscathed in the midst of storms.

We must now ascend the *calle alta*, which leads to the northern entrance. First appears the entrance itself, ornamented with the twelve Apostles, watching at the feet of Christ; then the cathedral apsis, with its two rows of windows, its buttresses, its bell turrets, the whole surrounded by an elegant balustrade, guarded at intervals by angels with unfurled wings, and whom an imaginative mind might easily suppose the true architects of this aerial cathedral, watching over and protecting it. The particulars we ~a e already mentioned would suffice to make it a beautiful church, but we have not yet mentioned the two ornaments which are its especial pride. On the right, where nave and transept intersect to form the cross, rises a large octagon tower, el Crucero, to the height of two hundred and thirty feet. It is lighted by two rows of windows, and from each of the eight angles is a smaller tower, carved, peopled with saints, and terminating in a slender spire. Behind the church, the cupola of the Constable's chapel—less elevated, but thoroughly octagon—reproduces the same decorations. These are the two diadems of this queen of Spanish basilicas. It is said that Charles V. at first sight of the Crucero was struck with admiration. "This jewel," said he, "must be put in a casket, and treated as some rare thing that one longs to have, but seldom sees." Most assuredly the passing stranger does not endorse this; but ravished with the spectacle, he cannot forbear applying to it these words, inscribed upon its façade in honor of the Blessed Virgin, "*Tota pulchra es et decora.*"

How willingly would we linger around these towers, or gaze enchanted upon the beautiful specimens of sculpture decorating the side door of the Pellegeria, or stop to admire the southern entrance, where a more ancient hand has depicted, in Byzantine style, the Eternal Judge, surrounded by the symbols of the four Evangelists! But it is time to cross the threshold, and the edifice whose elegance and grace resembled a jewel now becomes immense and seems a world.

But it is a world which God him-self fills, and indeed a divine symbol-ism has infused thought into these stones, or rather the power of awaken-ing thought, both in ourselves and the many generations who knelt here ages before us. It is the dogma of our re-demption, a Latin cross, which forms the plan of the edifice, whilst the mystery of the Holy Trinity presides over all the proportions: three naves the principal divided into nine gal-.eries, three for the vestibule, three

for the choir, three for the sanc-·
tuary. Indeed, as we advance
from the imposing portico to the
splendors of the apsis we seem to
behold the whole economy of the
Christian life typified in this edifice
Our first impression of the nave is
that of rare majesty, but a majesty
which strikes us as strained. We recognize the efforts of the Gothic art
to disengage itself from the Byzantine. The galleries are wide and low
and the massive arcade surmounting
them has no decorations save a few
sprays of trefoil. Were we to give
these walls language, they would
utter words of recollection and penitence, the first degrees of initiation
into Catholic truth, and in reality we

are now within the space appropriated by the rules of the ancient liturgy to penitents and catechumens.

At the fourth gallery commences the choir; on each side two rows of stalls, on which are represented, in beautifully carved workmanship, the principal scenes of the Bible and the legends of the saints. Elegant statuettes crown the wainscoting which relieves these naked walls.* But the choir is already flooded with the transept's brilliant light, even as the beams of

---

* The choir is now separated from the vestibule by a massive decoration which Cardinal Zapata had erected at the beginning of the seventeenth century, as a support to the archiepiscopal chair. This chair, of thoroughly classic work-manship, is carved to represent the capture of Europa.

contemplation succeed the laborious exercises of penance. Here, also, the light comes from above; it descends in a torrent through the octagon tower of the Crucero, whose exterior we have already admired. The interior has more majesty. Four pillars of a marvellous height sustain this great cupola, which is lighted by long arched windows, and decorated by bundles of ribs meeting at the summit, and forming a star which crowns the edifice, as the star of the Magi rested over Bethlehem's crib—the first, the poorest, and the holiest of cathedrals.

Still another degree in the mystic life, and the soul arrives at the most intimate union with its God. A few more steps and we reach the sanctuary, where Christ in the Eucharist perfects his alliance with humanity. The sanctuary of Burgos, exempt from wainscoting, opens to the sacred cere- monies a magnificent and luminous space. Six large silver candelabra decorate the altar steps. Behind, the altar-piece, reaching to the very roof, closes the perspective. The two Flem- ish painters who achieved this work wished it to proclaim the triumph of Our Lady, patroness of Burgos. Eleven bas-reliefs, in gilded wood, re- trace the Virgin's life from the nup- tials of St. Joachim and St. Anne to the coronation of the Queen of Heaven. But as if reminding us that her triumph, like that of every Christian soul, must be accomplished

through sorrow, all this is surmounted by the image of Mary at the foot
of the cross.    Large statues repre-
senting angels, the apostles, and the
evangelists, separate    the    bas-reliefs,
whilst the intervening spaces are filled
with . symbolic plants, enveloping in
their scrolls and tendrils the medal-
lions and names of a host of saints,
martyrs,    doctors,    pontiffs,    who    were
the glory of the Spanish church—St.
Vincent, St. Isidore, St. Dominic.    All
these great men are grouped around a
woman no less celebrated than themselves, and who lived at the very
time the altar-piece of Burgos was
designed—I mean St. Teresa.

If now the architect has not failed
in his mission, and these sermons of

wood and stone which greeted our entrance have accompanied us to the very sanctuary, growing more earnest and eloquent at every step, you will admire no longer; but, humbled and overcome, you will bend the knee in prayer, like the poor Spaniard telling his Rosary at your side. You have seen enough for one day.

But it is not so easy to have done with these grand Christian monuments.

When, after measuring with his steps the lateral naves, and contemplating the beautiful perspectives formed by the long arms of the Cross, one believes he has at last seen all the beauties of the cathedral, to his astonishment he perceives that there still remain to be visited a superb cloister and a long line of chapels, several of which have become like: so many churches around the principal edifice. Some contain many touching souvenirs, whilst others are noted for their rich altars and sepulchres. At Burgos, as in several of the grand Italian basilicas—for instance, at Venice, Padua, Florence—we never finish seeing, because Christian art never finishes creating. God himself reposed on the seventh day; he saw that his work was good and the perfect realization of his idea; but Christian art never reposes, because its productions fall infinitely short of the ideal.

I cannot forget the cloister, peopled with both the illustrious silent dead,

and the obscure but very noisy living.
Here we find statues of St. Ferdinand and his wife Beatrix; then a
long line of saints, bishops, and juris-
consults. At the same time we perceive a host of student lords buried
in their mantles, and repeating their
lessons aloud. Happily the lesson is
Latin, and should a few words chance
to reach the poor slumberers lying
here, they would still be unconscious
of the change of ages.

I shall not persuade you to visit all
these chapels—it would be equal to
Homer's enumeration of the Greek
fleet. But how can I pass unnoticed
St. Gregory's oratory, or that of the
Crucifix, with their beautiful legends?
The former contains St. Casilda's re-

lics, a patroness of old Castile, and whose history recalls the period when two religions, two peoples, lived in a perpetual struggle upon the same soil. Casilda was the only and beloved daughter of the Mussulman king who reigned at Toledo in the eleventh century. Being touched with compassion for the Christian captives who languished in the dungeons of her father's castle, whilst feasting and revelry filled the air, she secretly made them a daily visit, carrying concealed presents of wine and other nourishment. One evening, when met by the king, and urged to declare the contents of her robe, she answered, "Father, they are roses;" and letting fall the garment, behold, a shower of blossoms were scattered at her feet! In gratitude to their benefactress, the prisoners taught her to know Christ and his Mother. But an inflexible fatality seeming to debar her the gates of the church, God opened them by afflicting her with a malady that resisted every care and tenderness. At length she is warned in a vision that health will not be restored until she has bathed in the waters of Lake St. Vincent, near Briviesca, in a Christian land. The distracted father consents, and Casilda sets out on her journey as becomes a princess, attended by a numerous train, and loaded with presents for King Ferdinand I., then reigning in Burgos. Her reception is one in every way befitting that of a princess. Soon after

her arrival, plunging into the waters
of Lake St. Vincent, and emerging
from them vigorous and rosy, as had
been predicted, she demanded bap-
tism; after which, dismissing her attendants, she built herself a cell near
the lake, and there spent the remainder
of her days in works of penance.
Yearly, the 17th of April leads to
St. Casilda's hermitage all the laborers
and herdsmen of the neighboring mountains, who reverently gather the little
red stones scattered about these places
where the saint chastised her body,
believing them stained with her blood.

Do not shrug your shoulders at
these good people, or inveigh against
Spanish superstition; it is the human
element of their nature that makes the

Spaniards love these devotions appeal-
ing to the senses. For the Blessed
Virgin and the saints they have a tender veneration; but the ardor of their
piety centres in what is most spiritual
in Christianity—the sacrifice of Christ.
Hence, the number of soldiers, peasants, artisans, gentlemen of leisure,
who every day hear Mass at the Cathedral of Burgos; hence, also, the
crowd thronging the Chapel of the
Crucifix. The history of this crucifix
(*el santisimo Cristo de Burgos*) is no
doubt miraculous. Tradition attributes
it to the disciple Nicodemus, by whom
it was carved from the wood of a
plant not of earthly growth. After
many vicissitudes, the holy image, im-
pelled by wind and wave drifted from

the shores of Palestine into Biscay
Bay, where a merchant of Burgos
found it floating upon the waters.
Spanish piety has thrown around it the
halo of many prodigies; one of the
most touching I will relate. A golden
crown had been placed upon the head
of the Christ; but the holy head, de-
siring no other crown than that of
thorns, bent forward, and the rich diadem rested at its feet. Assuredly this
legend cannot fail to inspire devotion,
and whilst gazing upon the crucifix
in the midst of a prayerful multitude,
my lips murmured aloud the two following stanzas of an old poem which
expresses the sentiments of a Christian
heart: " God of immensity! thou who
never failest, who createdst the uni-

verse; thou true God, who from excess
of love for us didst expire upon the
cross: since thou wouldst suffer such
agony for our sins, O Lamb of God!
grant us a place with the good thief,
whom thou didst save only because he
said, ' Remember me.' *

We have reserved until now our
visit to the marvel of Castile—that
marvel of wealth and beauty to which
the traveller always devotes an hour,
has he but one to spend in Burgos—I
mean the Constable's Chapel, which is
cited as the type of the Spanish Renaissance, even as the English Renaissance has its in the chapel of
Henry VII. at Westminster. This

---

* These verses are those of Juan Tallante who
lived in the fifteenth century.

monument is so well known, pencil and
engraving have so popularized its beauties, that I almost feel dispensed from
attempting those indescribable details
which would leave the reader with only
a few confused ideas of the edifice,
when, in reality, I would wish to as-
tonish and delight him.  I shall merely
mention the characteristic features and
the names of its honored founders.  In
the year 1487, the Constable Hernandez de Velasco and his wife Doña
Mencia requested permission, as an
act of penance, to rebuild St. Peter's
oratory, which adjoined the cathedral
apsis.  The design of the new chapel
was octagon-shaped.  Exteriorly, it
harmonized with the cathedral, whose
principal ornaments it reproduced; in-

teriorly, it combined all the boldness of
the Gothic with the grace of the Spanish Renaissance. An arcade, ornamented with admirable bas-reliefs, and
the very grating of which is a master-
piece itself, conducts from the church
to the chapel. Having crossed this
vestibule, we suddenly find ourselves
under an elevated, luminous dome.
Slender colonnades mark the angles,
and rise up in a jet to the point where
they turn to enclose the arched windows, or form the eight-pointed star
that crowns the whole. Beneath the
windows open the galleries, proudly
surmounted by so many figures of
warriors, lance in hand. All around
hangs a festoon of stonework, surpass-
ing in beauty and delicacy the most

elaborate embroidery. This splendid decoration has nothing superfluous, it even leaves large naked spaces—legacies, no doubt, from the founders to the piety of their children. As to themselves, having accomplished their part, its founders repose in the centre of the noble edifice. The sub base of the mausoleum is only a block of marble, devoid of those decorations which enrich the sepulchres at Miraflores. But the figures of the Constable and his wife are beautiful, the armor and drapery wrought with rare delicacy. The sculptor's name is not given. I can learn only that the two statues were executed in Italy in the year 1542. The inscription reads: "Here lies the most illustrious Don

Pedro Hernandez de Velasco, Constable of Castile, and Viceroy of this country for their Catholic Majesties. He died in 1492, aged sixty-six. And with him lies the most illustrious lady Doña Mencia, Countess of Haro, daughter of Don Lopez de Mendoza and Doña Catalina de Figueroa, Marquis and Marchioness of Santillane. She died in the year 1500, aged seventy-nine." These two epitaphs unite the grandest names of the middle ages of Spain, names which seem with them to have descended into the tomb, but peacefully and gently. We recognize here as at Miraflores, both in monument and poet's song, the Castilian spirit as it sprang from the native soil, religious, chivalrous, pomp-

ous, but amiable and serene, reveal
ing no trace of that solemnity, that
sombre grandeur which it imbibed from
foreign climes, when the Austrian
princes, wishing to make Spain mis-
tress of the whole world, crushed her
beneath the burden.

And now the moment has come
when I must say adieu to these beautiful scenes I shall visit no more, and
to which I leave suspended a part of
those affections and regrets already
binding me to so many old cities,
mountains, and shores. A spot in
Sicily, where clusters of olive-trees
shade some broken columns; an oratory in the catacombs of Rome; at the
foot of the Pyrenees a chapel skirted
by limpid waters, stealing through

masses of tangled ivy, and the melancholy beach along the coasts of Bretagne, are all souvenirs of travel returning with infinite charm, especially when the present is sad and the future lowering. I shall add Burgos to these pilgrimages of thought, consoling the sorrowful pilgrimage of life. Suffer me, then, to take one last look at the cathedral. Let me kneel in this glorious sanctuary, before the Virgin of the altar-piece, and if the prayer of a Catholic scandalizes you, listen not.

"O Our Lady of Burgos! who art also Our Lady of Pisa and Milan, of Cologne and Paris, of Amiens and Chartres, Queen of all the grand Catholic cities, yes, truly you are beau-

tiful and gracious! *Pulchra es et decora*, since the thought of you alone
has clothed man's works with so much
grace and beauty.    Barbarians, they
left their forests rough and ferocious;
these incendiaries of cities seemed to
breathe only vengeance and destruction.  You rendered them so gentle
that they willingly obeyed masters,
and drew heavy loads to help build
your churches; so patient that they
considered as naught the ages spent
in carving your superb portals, galleries, and spires, so aspiring that the
height of their basilicas has far out-
stripped the most ambitious Roman
edifices, and at the same time so
chaste that all these grand architectural
creations with their host of marble

forms, breathe only purity and spiritual love. You have vanquished even the pride of these Castilians, who abhorred work as the sign of servitude; you have disarmed numberless hands whose only glory was in shedding blood, and giving them the trowel and chisel in place of the sword, for three hundred years have you retained them in your peaceful studios. O Our Lady! how God has rewarded the humility of his servant, and in return for the poor house of Nazareth where you lodged his Son, how many rich dwellings has he not bestowed upon you!"

A Christian lady who had also visited the Cathedral of Burgos, and often prayed in its sanctuaries, asks what God will do on the last day

with these admirable works erected
to his honor by the tender piety of
so many generations? Must that fire
which purifies the earth envelop in
destruction these towers that proclaim
his praises, these sacred arches guarded by angels, these pure Madonnas
and saints in humble adoration? And,
moreover, will He, who glories in being
called the Sovereign artist, destroy so
many mosaics and frescoes radiant with
eternal beauty? Why might not these
monuments also have their immortality
and their resurrection? Who knows
but what, miraculously saved, they will
one day ornament the New Jerusalem,
which St. John describes as resplend-
ent with jasper and crystal?

# VI.

THE wintry wings of winter have driven us off the road to Compostello, and our friends urge us not even to continue our route to Madrid. What! shall we come this far without taking a glimpse at Pampeluna and the gorges where the Basques boast of having defeated Charlemagne and his twelve knights? To be sure, my conscience is at ease in regard to Roland's pass, having actually seen the

breach which his sword made in the
neighboring mountain of Gavarnie,
and the two prints of his horse's feet
in the rock.

Unyielding prudence recalls us by
the shortest route. We are consoled,
however, on retracing our steps towards the north, to find ourselves gradually approaching a land of verdure
and sun. We have already redescend-
ed the rude passage of the Salinas.
It is Sunday morning, the smiling
valley resounds with bells and the
peasants, in joyous groups, are col-
lecting around the church-doors. Here
we see in all its freedom the spright-
liness and gayety of old Spain, and
the song of the muleteer or hotel
servant, that chances to greet us now,

is bright and sparkling. Even at
High Mass, in the principal church of
Tolosa, the organist treated us to a
very animated polka, yet the piety
of the faithful seemed in nowise
disturbed by this undevout music. I
saw all around me in profound adoration and fervent prayer stalwart,
handsome youths, equally capable of
handling a musket, or discussing the
*fueros* of the nation, and women has-
tening with their offerings, a white
loaf and a taper; whilst others, who
were widows, knelt upon a black car-
pet between two torches, and begged
prayers for their poor dead.

Our souvenirs of travel become
dearer, and our unwillingness to lose
an item greater in proportion as we

approach the frontiers.   How, indeed,
could we pass over in silence the
little village of Irun, which is an epi-
tome of modern, as Fortarabia's ruins
are of ancient Spain?   Here, then, is
the church of Irun, spacious and filled
with a devout multitude.   Under the
shadow of its spire is the parochial
school, whose refreshing tidiness might
tempt the most refractory urchin; then
the market, alive with active, cunning
peasants; now the palace of the governor, not devoid of elegance; before it, upon a graceful column, an
image of St. John the Baptist, patron
of the little city; and lastly, the pretty
white houses, a glimpse of whose
courts reveal the laurels and jasmines
of my dreams.   Oh! what a fine op-

portunity for a formal discourse whilst
the officials, with solemn slowness, in-
spect our passports. And why, in
times like these, when counsellors are
so numerous, should I refuse my ad-
vice to a nation whom I have known
eight days? I would tell Spain that
she has made a good, wise peace with
the Holy See, nobly defending its independence against the schemes of the
interested, who sought to place it under
tutelage, that she has taught nations
more experienced than herself how to
maintain the tradition of authority without stifling public liberty. It now remains for her to resume among the
Christian powers the grand part which
has been assigned her. Not in vain
does one of her coasts look towards

Italy; she is no longer to dream of conquests there, but neither must she permit this classic land to be over-run by invaders from the North. Another coast turns towards America, whose keys Christopher Columbus found, only to let them fall into the hands of oil and cotton merchants. In less than twenty-five years, Turkey repaired the disasters of Navarino; Spain cannot live always unmindful of Trafalgar's smoking ruins. And lastly, from her third coast she descries Af-rica, where the vanquished Alcoran vainly endeavors to reanimate the fana-ticism of its sectaries. The Spaniards justify their bull-fights as a school of courage which cultivates the mili-tary qualities of the nation. We have placed within their reach a better school of soldiers: the shores of Morocco are their promises, and their army needs no stronger stimulant than a union with that civilizing crusade which would make the Mediterranean a Christian lake.

But Spain hears me no longer. We are now at Behobia Bridge, where the two colors, Castilian and French, regard each other with the look of old acquaintances, who have met amidst powder and ball. Before touching the soil of France, and in gratitude to Our Lady for having brought us safely back, let me repeat an old canticle from the poet, Gil Vincent:

" Oh! how gracious is Our Lady,
Beautiful beyond compare!

"Tell me, hardy mariner,
    Whose home is on the sea,
    If ship, or sail, or wave reveal
    Aught beautiful as she?

"Tell me, armèd warrior,
    If to thine eye there be,
    In steed, or arms, or battle's din,
    Aught beautiful as she?

"Tell me, little herdsman,
    'Mid sun and flow'ret free,
    Seest thou in flock, in vale or mount,
    Aught beautiful as she?"

We began our pilgrimage with a
psalm; we finish with a canticle.

www.ingramcontent.com/pod-product-compliance
Lightning Source LLC
Chambersburg PA
CBHW030557040726
47497CB00008B/2773